As Far As
Mill Springs

As Far As Mill Springs

Patricia Pendergraft

PHILOMEL BOOKS
New York

Philomel Books, a division of The Putnam & Grosset Book Group,
200 Madison Avenue, New York, NY 10016
Published simultaneously in Canada
Book design by Sara Reynolds
The text is set in Cheltenham

Library of Congress Cataloging-in-Publication Data

Pendergraft, Patricia.
As Far As Mill Springs/written by Patricia Pendergraft.
p. cm.
Summary: Tired of being bounced from one foster home to another
during the Depression, twelve-year-old Robert embarks with his
friend Abiah on a long journey to find his mother, hoping to
reach her in time to celebrate Christmas with her.
ISBN 0-399-22102-6
[1. Depressions—1929—Fiction. 2. Foster home care—Fiction.
3. Christmas—Fiction.] I. Title.
PZ7.P3735Jo 1991
[Fic]—dc20 91-12318 CIP AC

First Impression

As Far As Mill Springs

Chapter One

From the table I could see the long branches of the Christmas tree jutting out just past the parlor door. They was full and green and looked like mystical fingers holding up the colored ornaments and tinsel that dripped from them like shimmering raindrops. The other kids was looking too. They was eight of us, four on one side of the table and four on the other, all twisting in our chairs and stretching our necks, trying to get a good gander at it.

They was Luther and Grady and Jimmy and Annie on the one side. And me and Abiah and Bertha and Laura on the other. We was all about the same age except for Abiah and Jimmy. They was the youngest. I reckon, except for fat Bertha who belonged to Phineas and Earlene Hickson who ran the home, and except for our hair and eye color, we all looked the same, as bedraggled as scarecrows left out in the winter weather. We wore flannel shirts and dark pants and scuffed-up brogans that was give to us by one of the charities in town. None of us was used to having anything so, when Christmas come, it was just like any day to us. I reckon we did get excited, though. I reckon Christmas excitement is just plumb built into a kid.

"CLOSE THAT DOOR, LUTHER!"

At the sound of old Phineas Hickson bellering out his command from down at the end of the table, we all snapped to attention, sat up stiff and straight in our chairs, and sent our eyes plunging down over our plates. Luther jumped up, almost knocking his chair over, and hurried to close the door and shut away the branches of the Christmas tree from our hungry eyes.

"Too much attention paid to folderal and not enough to serious matters such as thanking the Lord for our supper," Phineas bellered again while sending a scowling frown up and down each side of the table.

The door clicked closed and Luther come back to sit down at his place at the table. We snuck a quick look at each other, telling with our eyes how disappointed we was that we couldn't look at the Christmas tree no more. Soon we was all lowering our heads, listening to Phineas say grace. Before he could get to the part where he thanked the Lord for everything from his suspenders to the bounty of eggs the hens laid last spring, some of the kids commenced to snicker. But old Phineas was so wrapped up in the sound of his own voice that he didn't pay no attention. After a little, I felt a small pokey-poke against my ankle. I opened my eyes to a squint and seen Abiah Ringer was looking up under her eyelashes at me.

"That old sourpuss!" she whispered.

I poked her ankle back and said a soft "Sush!" and give Phineas a quick glance. He was at the part about the hens and eggs, so he didn't pay no mind.

Finally, when he said the last "Amen" he told Bertha to start serving the pertaters and Laura to serve the hot bread that Earlene had already cut into thin strips. Laura went around the table gingerly dropping the bread on all the plates and hurried to set back down in her chair. Bertha, like always, took her own time in getting to each one of us and, like always, they was never enough pertaters to go around. She was generous with some and stingy with others. When it come my turn to get a blob slapped into my plate, the bowl was near about empty.

"Oh, looky here," Bertha said, showing her fake concern with a nasty-nice look on her plug-ugly face. "They ain't no more taters. Not even a dollop!"

I squinted my eyes and glared at her close and hard, but she only sneered at me with a smirk of satisfaction. "Let me see!" I demanded under my breath so's old Phineas and Earlene, at the other end of the table, wouldn't hear. They was served first and was already lapping up their food like old billy goats going after tin cans.

The Hicksons and Bertha always got the most and best of everything. They'd took in homeless kids for so long they was knowed around town as "them good, charitable Christian folks who would take in any kid that was in need." What folks in the town of Temple didn't mention was, the Hicksons was being paid by the county for what they done for kids. Times was hard for everyone and some folks had plenty of nothing, but they was a few homes I heard of that was good to kids and even honest and fair. But the Hicksons sure weren't like that.

Me and all them other kids knowed different about them, all right. They wasn't a day went by we wasn't shoved around and punished for some reason or other. And, if they weren't no reason, old Bertha would make one up! They weren't a one of us kids in that home that wasn't made to feel like outcasts, homeless and living off the county, wearing hand-me-down rags and eating less than the Hicksons did. Right out to our face, they called us "foundlings" and "orphans" like we was nobody to bother much about, just motherless and fatherless kids they had to put up with. It sure was a strife being in *that* home, let me tell you.

After I told Bertha to let me see if they was any pertaters left, she shoved the bowl right up under my nose and twisted her mouth into a spiteful "Seeee."

Sure enough, they wasn't enough for one good dollop. Only a few white, buttery puffs of the pertaters clung to the sides of the bowl. While I studied the puffs, Bertha took her big fat finger and ran it along the inside of the bowl, gathering up the last little puffs, and shoved them into her mouth. Abiah, who had just a little old half blob of pertaters in her plate, leaned toward me and whispered, "Kick her! Kick her good, Robert!"

Abiah had been at the Hicksons' even longer than I had. She had come into the homes when she was just six years old. That was five years before the incidents I'm telling you about and plenty of time for her to learn to hate them. Her ma and pa and little sister was all killed in a car wreck only a mile from their farm. Abiah and her gran'ma was at the farm waiting for them to come down the roadway when a neighbor come instead, crying and telling them what happened. It weren't long after that her gran'ma passed on and they was no one left to raise her, nowhere for her to go but into the homes. She was the first one to speak to me when I come, which had been one year past and in the winter when the snow was piled high against the house and the nights was so cold it made you shiver right down to your bones. "You won't like it here," she said right off.

"Well, one more place don't make much difference," I told her. "I already been in eleven other homes and I didn't like them, neither."

"You *have?*" Abiah asked and her eyes got all round and big.

It was true. I'd been in homes since I was born, never did know who my ma and pa was ner why I was to be raised up the way I was. By the time I was put into the Hicksons' home by the county, I didn't expect nothing and I didn't get nothing, neither. After a while all I wanted was to get away from that awful place. I vowed it night and day and everytime I looked at old Phineas and Earlene and Bertha. And even though I liked all the kids in the home right well, I was tired of sleeping with Luther and having to listen to him snore all night and babble crazy things in his sleep and having Grady try to spook me about ghosts and Jimmy always making me feel bad, crying and carrying on about his ma and pa and having to look into Abiah's face and see the sadness in her eyes.

I heard over the years that my ma give me away when I was born, that she didn't want me and that I was passed on to home after home when I was little and didn't know what was going on. No one could ever tell me why my ma didn't want me and it come to me when I got some years on me not to ask anymore. They is some things a person has to find out for theirselves, I decided.

"I heard what you said!" Bertha snapped at Abiah and all at once she took the long wood spoon she'd been scooping up the pertaters with and hit Abiah right smack-dab on top of her head with it! Abiah cried out and rushed her hands up to the hit spot.

"What's going on down there?" Phineas called out, looking up from his filled plate and wiping his hand across his mouth to get the buttermilk out of his mustache. Phineas must of been nigh onto sixty years old or more. He walked with a stoop to his shoulders and had gray hairs all in his mustache and beard. He didn't have no hair on top of his head, though. His forehead was wrinkled and his skin was reddish looking. He'd been a woodcutter and outdoors most of his life before he decided to take in kids and get money from the county.

"Abiah is calling me names, Pa!" Bertha cried out with a faked look of hurt on her face.

"That ain't true!" I said, mad as I could be about such a lie. I'd come to feel sorry for Abiah and I didn't like the way Bertha treated her.

"You hush your mouth, Mr. Robert No-Name! No need to put *your* two cents in!" Old Earlene exploded with her fat jowls wobbling. She was about as fat as any woman I ever seen. Round as a barrel and short as a tree stump. With wide flat feet that run her shoes over on the sides. When she walked, it was with a "flump-flump" noise on the floor. When she called me "Robert No-Name" it was the closest thing to slapping me right across my face! There ain't nobody—even an orphan—who don't need a name.

"We'll have peace at this table or else!" Phineas threatened, shaking his fork in me and Abiah's direction. They was pertaters stuck on the end of the fork that fell off when he shook it.

"You'll be washing these dishes all by yourself tonight, miss!" Earlene went on, glaring over Abiah, who had her head down, looking at the little blob of pertaters and bread crumbs in her plate.

"And you, Robert, will be cutting wood for two hours this evening!" Phineas added like a trumpet horn, still shaking that fork at us.

I thought of how the wind was whipping at the shutters of the house, beating a howling path over the town, and of how even the cattle had been took in to keep them from freezing in the pastures. I didn't look forward to no two hours of chopping wood out in that kind of weather. But anything was better than being called Mr. Robert No-Name.

"Anyone else have anything to say?" Phineas trumpeted again, while running his suspicious eyes around the table at the rest of the kids. They all kept their mouths shut and their heads down.

Bertha made a little sound at my side, smiled a triumphant smirking smile at me, and moved on down along the table with the empty bowl.

"Bring me some more pertaters," Earlene told Bertha.

"They ain't none left in the bowl, Ma," Bertha said.

"Then go and get some more from out of the pan in the kitchen," Phineas grumbled as he tore into a piece of bread. Bertha scurried off to the kitchen.

I sure did wish I had me some of them pertaters in that pan out in the kitchen. I weren't looking forward to chopping wood on an empty belly no more than I was looking forward to doing it in the cold. I looked around at Abiah. Her head was still down and the ends of her short straight, dark hair hung over the sides of her face. I felt a strong tug of sorrow for her. Seemed like old man Phineas and that fat wife of his took more pleasure in punishing us kids than they almost did in eating. Most of the kids in the home was so beat down that you hardly ever heard them say a word except when the woman from the county come and asked how things was. Them times we got a bath and halfway clean clothes to wear. We never did other times.

After we et, Phineas told me to go to the bedroom all us boys shared and get my coat. "For you'll be at the woodpile, a mighty long time tonight," he added with some glee.

Down in the bedroom, I grabbed a piller and tossed it at Grady. It hit him across his back while he was bending over to get a book out of the tattered box on the floor by the bed. Someone give the Hicksons a bunch of books that they couldn't read and they give them to us boys. Grady could read right well and sometimes he read us stories out of them books. Stories you wouldn't never believe could really happen, but they was strong enough to make us close our eyes and believe for a while that we wasn't at the Hicksons' at all but off in some new land, discovering all kinds of wonderful things.

When the piller hit the floor, Grady swung around, looking mad as a hornet, grabbed it up from the floor and whammed me over the head with it. I tossed the piller to the floor and shoved old Grady down on the nearest bed. His long, muddy-colored hair fell out all around his face and his big gray eyes stared up at me in pure surprise.

"Think you're tough, don't you!" I said, laughing like a fool and I commenced to tickle him under his arms. When he started to howl, Luther jumped up on the bed, his blond curls dripping over his forehead. "Be quiet!" he hissed. "You want Phineas to hear us and have a bellering-fit?"

Right then Grady bit down hard on Luther's hand and Luther jumped off the bed with a shout, jumping up and down. I laughed even harder then.

"Quiet!" Jimmy cried, rushing to us from his bed. "Please be quiet! We'll all be sent to the cellar if you ain't." I looked around and saw the scared look on his face.

We stopped then. I let Grady go and Luther stopped howling and jumping up and down. We stood looking at each other, holding our breath, listening hard to hear if Phineas was coming to the door. After a while we breathed sighs of relief and I got my coat and pulled it on. It were an old coat someone give me in one of the homes I was in. It had thinned out over the years and was a might tight but it was all I had to do me.

"I hated it when he wouldn't let us look at the Christmas tree. I didn't want to shut the door." Luther said like it was an apology.

"What difference does it make? We ain't got no presents under the tree, anyway," Grady said with a snort.

"The girls has got some. I seen them," Jimmy said. Then he frowned. "I didn't see none for Abiah, though."

"They're mostly all for Bertha," Luther put in. "Abiah ain't got none because her and Bertha is always into it."

"It ain't Abiah's fault!" I said in a disgusted voice and I buttoned my coat and pulled on my bill cap. The cap wouldn't keep the wind all the way out of my ears and the coat wouldn't keep me warm enough, but if I chopped the wood hard enough, I might work up a warm sweat. I started for the door and reached out and touched the top of Jimmy's head on the way. He looked up at me.

"Maybe someday someone will come and adopt us and take us away."

"Don't count on it, Jimmy. Better just face facts. Kids like us has got to take all the knocks in life." I opened the door and walked out into the hall, wishing I hadn't told Jimmy that. But I reckoned he ought to know the truth. Not only did we have to take the knocks, we couldn't really trust no one neither.

Chapter Two

I'll get away from here somehow," I vowed again as I stood out in the cold wind chopping the wood. Each time I sent the ax thudding down into the wood, I said it over and over in my mind and out loud too. "Won't even let us kids get a good gander at the Christmas tree . . . didn't even put nothing under the tree for Abiah . . . not even enough pertaters to eat. . . ."

Finally, when I was plumb wore out, I stabbed a log in the middle with the ax, stood for a minute rubbing my hands together to get them warmed up, then set down on the end of the log to rest. While I set there huddled down in my coat, I commenced to think about how it would be to live in a real home, with my own folks, have a bed of my own and presents under a beautiful, bright Christmas tree. But mostly, I thought about my ma and pa, wondering for the thousandth time if they was dead or alive and if they ever thought about me. I wished I could be with them, no matter where they was, on this Christmas especially. I'd be thirteen years old on Christmas Eve, coming into my teens, growing up and never even knowing what my ma and pa looked like, who I took after, ner what my last name was.

I commenced to feel inside me just how it would be between me and my ma and pa. If we was ever to be together, we'd make up for all twelve years I hadn't been with them. I'd be their Christmas present and they'd be mine and when they asked, and surely they would, if I forgave them for giving me away, I'd throw my arms around both of them and shout, "Why, *sure* I do!"

Maybe they would be all alone and not even have a Christmas tree. I'd cut one down for them. I'd go out into the woods and find the best old fir tree I could and I'd bring it in the house and we'd decorate it together with shining tinsel and angel's hair. Ma and Pa and me, we'd be the carols and music and laughter and fruitcake and hot jelly buns and Christmas pudding! Why, me and Ma and Pa, we'd be everything to each other.

Well, no sense in thinking about that, I decided abruptly as I stood up and pulled the ax out of the log and went to chopping at it fast and hard. No sense in thinking about nothing but getting away from the Hicksons' place. "No sense at all . . ." I said as I split the log in two and grabbed up another one. Somehow I couldn't keep the thoughts of Ma and Pa out of my mind though, and the harder I chopped, the stronger the feeling come about them. I reckon I would of froze out in the weather if it hadn't been for my thoughts. Them two hours suddenly started to fly.

I finished cutting the wood and got it stacked in the old lean-to shed beside the house. I'd worked up a sweat and two sore arms, but I felt plenty warm enough. When I got the last log stacked, I stood next to the house and looked out into the night. It was cold and the wind was sweeping like a broom across everything, but it was clear and the stars was bright and I didn't want to go back into the house. I decided to take a little walk down the road and ended up where a lot of pinecones had fallen to the ground. Some of them was small and well shaped and, for some reason, I thought about Abiah and how she didn't have no present under the Hicksons' Christmas tree. I leaned down and picked up a couple of the smallest pinecones and looked them over as well as I could in the darkness. They seemed perfect in every way. I shoved them into my pocket and walked back to the house and stood at the edge of the yard, staring into the winder.

The curtains was drawn back and the Christmas tree sang out through the winder like a Gospel song sung by a hundred voices, the wondrous sound slipping down through a bright sunlit sky. I blinked my eyes over and over. It was mystery and magic and I commenced to ache inside just to look at it. It was so big and green and perfect. The lowest branches was like a wide, ballooning skirt that just touched the tops of the bright packages beneath it. Then it grew narrower as my eyes traveled up it. At the very top was a gold star with tinsel dripping from it and falling into the highest branches. Ornaments of all colors and sizes was hung on every branch and small lights sent shades of blue and red and yeller into the white angel's hair that wound all through the green branches.

I thought all of a sudden how that tree and all them beautiful trimmings was give to the Hicksons for the enjoyment of all us kids and they was denying it to us. I started to shake, I was so fired up with mean anger. The old *devils!* I touched the pinecones in my pocket with my fingers and thought about Abiah again. "You'll get your present,

Abiah," I vowed to the cold night and I started across the yard to the house. "I swear you will!"

Before I reached the front doorway, I seen old Phineas standing there watching me. "Get in here, you little scamp! You better of got all that wood cut!" he warned me.

"Yes, sir, I did, sir," I said real polite as I rushed through the door past him.

From the front door, I hurried through the house and through the door of the damp, high-walled bathroom. I reckoned I ought to at least wash off the pinecones for Abiah. As I held them under the water in the sink, my eye was drawn away to something on the floor. I put my head down and stared. It was a ribbon. A short, shining, pretty yeller ribbon laying on the floor near the feet of the rusty old bathtub. I shut off the water and dried the pinecones on a towel that was throwed across the side of the tub. Then I bent down and picked up the ribbon and, as I did, I had an idea. If I tied the pinecones together with the ribbon, it would make a special, nicer present for Abiah. She could even use the ribbon in her hair, if she wanted to, and set the pinecones out somewhere in the girl's bedroom to look at all the time. I got a big grin on my face just to think about the look that would come over Abiah's sad-eyed face when she seen the pinecones all tied up with the pretty ribbon.

It didn't take but a minute to tie the pinecones together. When I finished, I opened the door slowly and peered out. I could hear Grady and the other boys down in the bedroom playing dominoes and the girls in their bedroom talking in low voices. There weren't no one in the hallway. I hurried out the door and skittered along the wall like a creeping cat, clutching the pinecones tightly in my hand. When I reached the kitchen, I hurried through it, then into the dining room where I listened at the parlor door, making sure there was no voices in the room. It was still and silent on the other side. I glanced around behind me then opened the door and went inside. The Christmas tree lights had been turned off and the fire in the fireplace put out. The room was cold and filled with the fragrance of the Christmas tree. I went right to it and bent down to place the pinecones in an open spot between two small packages where Abiah was sure to see it. "It's yours, Abiah," I would tell her on Christmas morning. I had to grin again just to think about the happy expression on her face.

All at once they was a click at the door and I jerked around. Bertha was standing there, her hands on her hips, a pinch-mouthed, accusing look on her face. I jumped up and tried to shove past her.

"I seen what you done," she said and she rushed to the tree. In an instant she had Abiah's present in her hands.

"Put that back!" I said, trying to keep my voice low, but I was so furious just to think that Bertha even touched it that I could feel my voice rising into a shout when I said, "It ain't for you!"

"It is too! This is *my* yeller ribbon!" Bertha shouted back.

"You leave it be!" I said in a hard, even voice as I bounced toward her. She stood up and put her hands behind her and yelled to the top of her lungs for her ma.

I could hear old Earlene's flat-footed, run-over shoes slapping at the floor before she even reached the parlor. When she finally appeared, she was wiping her hands on her flour-sack apron and licking her lips together like she'd just finished eating again. She glared at me right off like I'd committed a crime.

"Ma, Robert stole my hair ribbon!" Bertha cried as soon as she seen Earlene.

"I did *not* steal it!" I defended myself. "It was on the bathroom floor, just laying there and . . ."

"You knowed it weren't yourn!" Earlene spit at me with her eyes narrowed hatefully over me.

But it's for Abiah, I wanted to tell her. It's because Abiah ain't got nothing under the tree. It's because you mean old Hicksons give Bertha lots of presents and the other girls got some too. Only Abiah ain't got nothing and it ain't fair! I wanted to say all them things, but before I could get it all arranged in my mind, Bertha pulled her hands out from behind her back and Earlene got a gander at the pinecones tied up with the ribbon. She made a little noise of pleasure down in her throat and said, "Why, that's a good idea, tying them little cones together with your ribbon, honey."

"She didn't do it!" I insisted.

"You hush your mouth!" Earlene warned me and she took the pinecones from Bertha and shoved them down into her apron pocket. Then she looked at Bertha and smiled. "Let's gather up some more of them little cones tomorrow. They ought to make some nice decorations for our Christmas supper table."

Bertha looked at me and smiled her hateful, satisfied smile and I couldn't keep from crying out, "I *won't!* I *won't* hush up!" I shouted so loud that some of the kids from the bedrooms come and poked their heads around the door to see what was going on. When Earlene raised her head back and exploded with, "PHINNNNNEEEEAAAASSS!" they all scattered.

In an instant, Phineas was there, his hands on his belt, demanding to know what was going on.

"We have a thief here," Earlene answered, giving me a glance. "He stole Bertha's nice decoration and claims it's his."

"I didn't steal it, sir," I spoke up and my voice was trembling.

"He did too, Pa! I made that decoration for Ma's Christmas table!" Bertha lied, looking her pa right in his eyes.

Earlene took the pinecones out of her apron pocket and held them for Phineas to see. After he had inspected them, sniffed a little, and gripped his belt a little tighter, he turned to me and said, "Well, Robert, which will it be, the belt or the cellar?"

I refused to open my mouth. I latched my top teeth over my bottom ones and ground them in. They could all stand there and beg me till doomsday, if that's what they was a mind to do, but I wasn't going to give them no satisfaction in an answer.

"Better give him the cellar," Earlene said finally. "Reverend Shamlin will be coming. It wouldn't look good to have whelps on the boy."

Phineas agreed with a nod of his head. "All right, Robert, head for the cellar."

I looked at Bertha with all the hatred I had stored inside me. How could she do such as this? I wondered. But even more than hating Bertha, I felt a deep pain in my heart for Abiah. I walked out the door and heard Phineas walking behind me. I'd have to have my punishment for what I didn't do, down in that old cold, dark cellar with all the rats and mice and spiders, whether I liked it or not.

Chapter Three

The cellar weren't new to me. I'd been down there before. All the boys had, for some stupid reason or another that didn't amount to a hill of beans. We all feared it. But I learned to endure it.

As we went down the steps, me in front of Phineas with him carrying the flickering lantern, I pried my teeth apart and asked him how long my stay in the cellar was going to be.

"Till morning," he answered gravely.

Well, I thought, that would give the rats just about enough time to go to nibbling on me! When we reached the cellar door, Phineas stepped around in front of me and opened it. The cold, dank, musty air flew out at me and I could smell the mice and rats nesting in all the dark, hidden places.

"You'd best do some heavy thinking on mending your ways while you're down here," Phineas said and he stepped back, waited for me to enter the door, then he pulled the door closed and with it all the light.

I stood there for a minute, calculating where the old rickety bench was that I always sat on and how far away from it the closest scratchy noise from the rats' nest was. "Y'all come on out! Here's your supper!" I called in a half-scared voice, but I didn't hear no movement ner nothing so I went in the direction I recalled the bench was in and eased myself down on it. But I soon got back up and started going round and round in circles. It was the only way to keep warm and the only way to keep the varmits off me.

As I walked I thought about Abiah and the present I'd made for her. I wanted to cry but I couldn't. Instead I commenced to think of how I would get away from the home. I decided the sooner the better. I'd leave the Hicksons and head out looking at the country. I'd keep going until I'd seen all there was to see. By then I'd be growed up enough to maybe look for my ma and pa.

In a corner I heard the sound of the rats beginning to scratch. I shivered with fear, but they wasn't nothing I could do about it. Finally I sat back down on the bench and as soon as I did, I heard a skittering noise and a "tink" sound like glass hitting glass and suddenly there was a crash on the floor. It had to be one of Earlene's jars of preserves or vegetables and a rat had to of knocked it off the shelf! I layed back on the bench, making sure my feet and legs wasn't falling over the sides and made up my mind I just as well try and relax. The night would be long, but maybe the rats would eat whatever was in that broken jar instead of me.

I couldn't remember sleeping, but I opened my eyes to the sound of voices coming through the cellar door, so I reckoned I had slept. I reached down first thing and felt my feet. They was still there with my legs attached. The rats had missed me again. I started hearing footsteps connected to the voices outside the door and I sat up.

"We've got a problem with the boy, Reverend Shamlin. Lies and steals. Ornery as a cuss. We don't know what to do with him half the time. He's a real trial for us." It was old Earlene yapping.

"I heard his father was the same way. Always in some kind of something. Could be the boy comes by it naturally." As soon as I heard Reverend Shamlin's voice and the mention of my pa, I scatted over to the door so's I could hear more.

"Who was the daddy?" Earlene asked.

"A young lout, so full of spit and vinegar, the mother left him straightaway. The boy's been all over the county in different homes all his life."

"What happened to the mother, do you know?" Earlene went on and I squashed my ear flat against the door and listened with all my might.

"She married again. That I know. I knew her as a young girl. Pretty and lively, she was. She married a Whitlaw over in Beal County after the first marriage didn't work out. They moved away shortly after to a place called Mill Springs. It's up-country aways."

"Well, she's well rid of the boy!" Earlene said with a smack of her lips that I could hear clear through the door.

As soon as I heard the footsteps start again I jumped away from the door like a firecracker going off and sat down on the bench to wait. Mill Springs . . . married a Whitlaw . . . father full of spit and vinegar . . . Mill Springs . . . up-country aways . . . I heard the words of the Reverend spinning round and round in my head.

I was still in a daze when the door opened and Earlene and Reverend Shamlin walked through it. "I won't stay, Reverend. You visit with the boy alone," Earlene said and she handed the Reverend the lantern in her hand without even looking in my direction, turned, and walked out of the cellar.

Reverend Shamlin walked toward me carrying the lantern and set it down on the bench. He sat down on the other side of it. The bench creaked and snapped when his weight sunk onto it. I could see his face in the lantern light looking round and pink from the cold air. He looked as old as Phineas, but they weren't a trace of meanness in his face like old Phineas had. The Reverend had a kind face, solemn eyes, and a bush of white hair that matched the color of the white collar he wore that peeked out above his dark suit.

"Well, Robert, what have you done to be put down here in this cellar?" he asked me, looking right into my eyes.

"I ain't done nothing bad, Reverend Shamlin," I answered right up.

"'Nothing' didn't put you here, son."

"What good would it do me to tell you, sir? You'd believe them any time before you'd believe me." I didn't keep no secret about my feelings from Reverend Shamlin.

"You must learn to respect your elders, Robert, and to obey them. You must learn to live in peace, have humility, have . . ."

I sure could feel a Sunday sermon coming on!

"I beg your parden, sir, but what about them Hicksons?"

"The Hicksons are a fine family, Robert. They have taken in and raised many homeless children over the years."

"And got paid for it, too," I blurted out.

"That doesn't make them any less what they are: a good, God-fearing man and woman who are giving compassion and care to those who are less fortunate."

"It ain't fair, what they done to me."

"You are causing your own suffering, Robert, and casting dark shadows of misery and pain over this house."

I gulped hard at that and looked deeply through the lantern light at the Reverend's face. It seemed to of turned from kind to stern. Me, casting shadders? What Reverend Shamlin didn't know or didn't want to know, was that the Hicksons theirselves was the shadders. The way they treated all the kids was what they called in church an "abomination." I couldn't understand how they had hid their true selves from everyone for so long.

"Robert," the Reverend said.

"Yes, sir."

"I want you to bow your head and repeat something after me."

"What is it?"

"It's from the Bible."

I didn't feel too comfortable about it, but I bowed my head anyway. I reckoned it was the Reverend's job and what he was called on to do, praying over folks and such, so I bowed my head and waited.

The Reverend cleared his throat huskily, like he was getting ready to say a big Sunday sermon. I glanced up at him under my eyelashes. His eyes was closed tight as a jug.

"Put on then, as God's chosen ones, holy and beloved . . ." he commenced and it was my turn to clear my throat. ". . . compassion, kindness, lowliness, meekness, and patience, forbearing one another . . . " His voice was low and solemn and I recognized the verse from all them Sunday schools I'd been forced to attend over the years.

I repeated the words as best I could, but when he come to that word "forbearing," I wondered just how long I was going to have to "forbear" them no-good Hicksons.

"Why did you stop, Robert?" the Reverend asked and I looked up and he was looking down at me. Shadders fluttered all around his head from the lantern.

"Well, sir, I was just thinking that I done forbeared enough in this place. And I was wondering if I could be tooken to another place to live. Maybe one where I wouldn't have all this durned forbearing to do all the time."

Reverend Shamlin raised his shoulders back and looked down his short, squat nose at me. "Robert!" he breathed like he was shocked, and all at once he took the back of my head in his hand and shoved it down and started speaking again. He'd say a few words and rattle my head, meaning for me to say the words after him. "Forbearing one another and forgiving one another, if any man have a quarrel against any, even as Christ forgave you, so also do ye." When he was finished and I was done repeating after him, he slipped his hand away from my head and said, "You must ask your father in heaven to forgive your bad feelings for the Hicksons, Robert."

"Yes, sir," I said real quick, just to shut him up.

"Good," he said as though he was satisfied. He picked up the lantern and stood up.

I was itching to ask him about my ma, about all I'd heard him tell Earlene outside the cellar door. Things like how old she would be now, how come her to give me up but, when I started to mention it, he turned away from me and walked to the door. I could see he was anxious to get out of that musty old cellar, same as I was. I jumped up and follered him.

"How much longer will I have to stay down here, sir?" I asked, looking up into the brightness of the lantern and the way it glowed over his face.

"I will go out and tell the Hicksons you want to ask their forgiveness . . ." he started and I yanked at his arm.

"But I don't want to do that!"

He turned and looked down at me. "You *must* do it!" he said and his expression told me if I ever wanted to be let out of that awful cellar, I'd better do it.

"Yes, sir," I said and I hung my head and wondered who had the best life, them rats and mice that lived in that terrible hole of a cellar, or me who had to live with them no-good Hicksons!

Reverend Shamlin opened the door and the light from the top of the stairs shone through to the cellar. We began to slowly climb the stairs. When we reached the top, Phineas was standing there, looking as big and as menacing as some giant, staring down at me with a deep frown on his face.

"We didn't expect you to bring the boy up, Reverend," he said, like he didn't agree with Reverend Shamlin's actions.

"Robert has something to say to you, Phineas," the Reverend said and he turned to look at me, his eyes coaxing me to speak.

I cleared my throat and dug the toe of my ragged shoe into the dirty, splintery step. "I . . . I want to . . . to apologize to you, sir, for . . . for what I done and . . . and causing you t–trouble," I said and I would of ruther et a raw mouse than have to say it!

Old Phineas squared his shoulders back and said, "Well now, that's more like it, boy." And to Reverend Shamlin he said, "Well, I see you put the fear of the Lord in him."

They walked ahead of me and disappeared around the turn to the kitchen. As I started to take the first step off the stairway, I looked up and there was Bertha with a big mean-looking smile on her face.

"You have to apologize to me too!" she said as she crossed her heavy arms over her fat chest.

It didn't take much for me to see that Bertha meant what she said. But there weren't no way I was going to say I was sorry to her! "I ain't got nothing to apologize to you for!" I told her with my temper boiling.

"Oh, yes you have. You stole my hair ribbon, don't forget," she said with a mean-looking smile.

"I didn't *steal* it!"

Suddenly that mean smile left her face and her hands flashed out in front of me, giving my shoulders a hard shove, and down the stairs I went, backwards!

"Pa! Pa! Robert fell down the stairs!" I heard her yell as I tumbled and bounced head over heels to the bottom of the steps.

When I landed, I laid there just to see if I was broke apart or if I was all together, like before Bertha pushed me. I was sore and my head ached from hitting the steps, but I reckoned I was going to be able to stand. The next thing I knowed, Earlene was calling for Grady and Luther to run down the stairs and help me up. They did, and when I stood, feeling dizzy at first, I looked up to the top of the stairs and seen

Bertha standing there with her big mean smile looking down at me. Sure as hell, I was going to have to forbear Bertha till I could somehow get out of that house!

That night, just after the lights was out and everyone was supposed to be in bed, they was a small knock on the boys' bedroom door. I got up and went to it, fearing it might be Bertha up to another trick against me. But when I opened the door, I seen in the dimness that it were Abiah, standing there in her nightgown.

"Thank you, Robert," she whispered and all at once I felt her wet lips on my cheek!

I reached up and touched the spot, feeling embarrassed. But I managed to ask, "For what?"

"The girls told me about the present you made for me."

"But you didn't get it."

"I got the thought. Ain't that what counts most?" she said and turned to hurry back down the hall to the girls' bedroom. When I left that place the only person I would miss would be Abiah.

Chapter Four

Mill Springs . . . Mill Springs . . . that was where my ma lived. And she was married to someone else. A Whitlaw. I felt a tug of disappointment that her and my pa wasn't married no more. But I couldn't do nothing about that. All I could do now was study on finding Ma. At least I knowed the name of the place she was. Reverend Shamlin had told Earlene she was pretty. But that didn't tell me what she looked like. I wondered deep and hard about that and what she sounded like and what she did all day long and if I ever crossed her mind. I commenced to think about getting to her every minute just about. It was more important to me than food even.

The next day after I was took out of the cellar, while me and Luther and Phineas was out chopping more wood to store in the shed, I watched the old duffer like a hawk, waiting for a time when I could ask him a question about Mill Springs. I didn't want him to get suspicious. I had to be careful about that. Finally a time come when he looked all wore out and laid his ax down to rest a spell.

"Sir," I said and cleared my throat so loud Luther, carrying an armful of wood to the shed, turned and looked at me.

"Sir," I started again. He was already staring at me from the throat clearing. "Where you reckon Mill Springs is? You reckon it's near here?" I started gathering up kindling from the ground just to look busy and pretend my question to him weren't all that important.

Phineas ran the sweat off his forehead with the back of his big red hand and squinted his eyes at me. "Oh, 'bout as far as the crow flies," he answered. "How come you to ask?"

"Ain't no special reason," I answered, but I was plenty disappointed in his answer. After a minute I said, "Sir, how far does a crow fly?"

He eyed me hard and snarled, "Pick up that ax and get busy!" Then he mumbled something to hisself and walked off.

When Earlene called us in for supper, I kept a watch out for a curious stare from Phineas. But he was too busy rounding up the kids and herding us to the table to pay me any mind.

At the table, Bertha was her usual ornery self, making faces at me and shorting Abiah and me both on the pertaters. When she went to serve Abiah she "accidentally on purpose" nudged into her with the pertater bowl and cried out, "Oh, I'm sorry, Abby!" There was a mean smile behind what she said.

"I done *told* you a hundred times! *My name ain't Abby!* It's *Abiah!* It's all I got of my own and *I ain't going to let no one take it away from me!*"

When I seen Abiah start to get up out of her chair, I jumped up and shoved her down. I knowed she'd be put into the cellar if she laid a hand on Bertha.

"What in tarnation is going on here?" Phineas bellered out.

"Robert's going to hit me, Pa!" Bertha answered with her face all crinkled up and she backed away from me just like I was about to. Around the table, all the kids was watching like they was holding their breath.

"Always a sign of contention! Always into trouble! Can't get along with nobody!" Earlene grumbled to Phineas.

Phineas stood up and leaned over the table. "What's got into you, boy? You ain't learned nothing, have you! I reckon the Reverend was too easy on you, let you out of the cellar too soon."

"Ain't nothing to do but send him back to the cellar and leave him there till all that fire is put out in him," Earlene said and all the fat on her was shaking with anger.

I felt a fierce, stinging hatred overtake me. Go back into that cellar with them durned varmits and spiders and the cold? I started to shake, I was so filled with fury. I'll *never* go back in that cellar, I vowed to myself as I stared into Phineas' blazing mad eyes.

From the corner of my own eyes, I seen Abiah stand up. "No!" I said and I turned to give her a full look. Her eyes was dark and big and I could see that she was afraid. "Sit down!" I hissed at her. But she wouldn't. She stood there looking at me until Phineas thundered, "Lord, God! What have we got here? Another heathern child?"

"Yes! Yes, you have!" Abiah cried in a trembling voice.

"*Be quiet!*" I said and I tried to push her back into her chair, but she wouldn't budge from my side.

All the kids was so quiet you couldn't hear a one of them sniff or scrape their forks across their plates. It seemed like they waited in fear for something dreadful to happen. And it did.

"Sinful little heatherns!" Earlene bellered as she got up from the table and rumbled fatly toward me and Abiah. When she reached us she grabbed Abiah's arm and shoved her in the direction of the kitchen. "You'll be washing all the pots and pans and scrubbing the kitchen floor while we eat, young lady. Then you'll wash the supper dishes and you won't get a morsel of food until tomorrow!"

Abiah looked back at me as she stumbled through the kitchen doorway with Earlene behind her. Phineas got up and stormed toward me with his eyes cutting through me like a saw. "And you, you ungrateful little devil, will be spending the night in the cellar!"

No, I won't! I said inside myself. I won't *never* spend another minute down there! I could feel my blood go blazing hot in my veins, I was so hungry to get a lick in on Phineas. But he grabbed my arms and held them behind my back and started pushing me ahead of him. I wiggled and twisted, trying to get loose, but I couldn't. Suddenly a mellow, sweet-sounding voice came trilling through the house from the front door and Phineas let me go with a swift shove and a hiss for me to set down.

"Yoo-hoo!" the voice sang out again and Phineas made a dash for the kitchen and the next thing that happened was, Earlene come rushing out looking as mean as forty mad dogs, nudging Abiah ahead of her to her chair and pushed her down in it. As soon as Abiah hit the chair, in walked Lottie Shamlin, the Reverend Shamlin's wife, with a bright smile on her pretty face.

"Good evening all," she said cheerily. "I took the liberty of walking right in the front door. I hope you don't mind. The wind was so cold I felt I couldn't wait a minute out on the steps."

"Why, of course you couldn't, Miz Shamlin," Earlene said, with her mad dog look replaced by a friendly smile. And Phineas added with his own picture-perfect smile, "You're always welcome with or without a knock on the door, you know that, Miz Shamlin. They ain't a soul that follers the Lord's way that would ever be turned away from our door."

My belly ached when I seen them smiles and heard the way the Hicksons talked to Miz Shamlin. Me and all the kids run our eyes around the table at each other.

"I just stopped by to leave this basket filled with a few gifts and goodies for the children. We took up a little monetary collection in the church as well. Not much, mind you, for it's hard times we're having this winter, but enough so that each child will have a few pennies to spend for Christmas." Miz Shamlin set the basket down on the table between Jimmy and Annie and give them each a warm smile and a pat on their heads with her gloved hand. "Bless all their little hearts," she said and, looking back up at Earlene and Phineas, she added, "How wonderful it is that they have you two to care for them."

The smiles that rose like beams of sunlight across Phineas and Earlene's faces at what Miz Shamlin said made me want to jump up and shout the truth of that place and that old couple. But I didn't. Instead I looked around the table, at the smirks of disbelief on the faces of all the kids, that no one knowed what went on inside that house.

Then I looked at Abiah. She was staring at Miz Shamlin like she hadn't never seen anyone so pretty. Miz Shamlin was pretty, all right. She had the whitest, clearest skin I ever seen and reddish hair with specks of gray in it, parted in the middle and partly covered by the hood of her cloak. I wondered if she looked anything like my ma.

"It was our calling many years ago to take in foundlings and orphans," Phineas spoke up with his chest shoved out proudly.

"The Lord spoke to us in nineteen and twenty-five, telling us what He wanted us to do and we've tried to abide by our Christian duty ever since," Earlene added, then she cast her eyes down like she was timid about tooting her own horn.

"I'll set a spell if you don't mind," Miz Shamlin said, pushing the hood of her cloak all the way off her head. "It's so cold, my bones seem to have caught a chill. But you go on eating, please." She sent another kind smile around the table to us kids.

"We're ready to have some hot cocoa, Miz Shamlin. The young'uns will clear the table and all the girls will work together washing up the dishes and cleaning the kitchen, just like they always do," Earlene said and I give Abiah another look. She was off the hook about doing the kitchen work by herself. Leastways for the time Miz Shamlin was there. But what about me? I wondered.

All at once my question was answered. "You boys go out and bring in more wood for the fireplace, then you can play dominoes like you always do," Phineas said like a kind father would, and he give me a small, mean glance and I knowed I was off the hook too.

I breathed a sigh of relief as the three of them left the room and went into the parlor to sit down. All along the table, up and down, I could see the faces of the other kids relax, like as if one big sigh had passed through all of them at the same time.

Us boys went out and got the wood from the woodshed while the girls cleared the table and not a word passed between a one of us. After we got the wood set on the hearth in the parlor and started to leave, Miz Shamlin, who was setting in a chair close to the fireplace said, "Do let the boys stay a minute. The Christmas tree looks so lovely and they must be almost frozen from being out in the cold."

Phineas cleared his throat and him and Earlene exchanged a private disgusted look. "The children do take pleasure in the tree," Earlene said.

Me and Luther and Grady and Jimmy sure got a firecracker blast out of that! But we was already staring at the Christmas tree. The lights was lit and glowing in the angel hair and the star at the top looked all bright and shining from the fire in the fireplace. Seemed like we was just beginning to drink it all in when Phineas cleared his throat again and said, "The boys has some little chores to do in their room. They've looked at this tree day and night till it's about wore out from being seen." It was the first time we'd ever got a good gander at it.

"Oh," Miz Shamlin said. "Good night then, young men, and Merry Christmas."

"Merry Christmas, Miz Shamlin," we all said in unison.

We walked silently to the bedroom and sat down at the table where the domino game was set up. We sat down, but no one felt like playing. I reckoned they was a pure sick feeling in all of us from the play-acting the Hicksons done for Miz Shamlin's benefit. All at once Jimmy laid his head on the edge of the table and commenced to cry. We looked at him, at his dirty blond hair and shoulders that shook as his muffled sounds fell out into the room, but they was no way to comfort him. Seemed like he just had to get it out. He was like me, shunted around from pillar to post for so long, he didn't know who he was ner what he was doing in all them strange places he'd had to live. Me and the other boys just sat there, staring at Jimmy's dirty hair.

It weren't much later that we heard Miz Shamlin getting ready to leave and Phineas telling her he would drive her home in his old rattletrap car. I listened and waited and wondered what I was going to do. It was certain, I weren't never going to be punished by Phineas Hickson again.

Chapter Five

As soon as the front door closed, old Earlene was out in the dining room going through the basket Miz Shamlin had brought. All of us kids could hear her pilfering around in the stuff, mumbling and smacking her lips with "oh" and "ah" sounds. After a little we heard Bertha rattling through things with her. Me and Luther left the bedroom, snuck to the doorway of the dining room, and peered inside.

"Vulters! Look at them!" Luther whispered to me.

I knowed I ought to of believed what I seen and heard, but it sure was hard to accept as true. Luther seen it too and heard every word, so I know it were true and I wasn't just thinking it all up in my head.

Earlene and Bertha was pulling all the bright bows and wrapping paper off the little packages they took out of the basket and opening them up so fast, the paper and bows was flying in all directions.

"We'll keep these here socks and that pair of mittens for you, Berthie," Earlene said as she ripped through another package. "And here's a pair of earmuffs. Your pa could use a new pair, cold as it is. Now, where is that money Miz Shamlin said folks collected for them little heatherns?" I reckon it weren't enough they had tooken the present I made for Abiah. Now they had to steal from all the kids!

"Here it is, Ma," Bertha said and she lifted up a small round handkerchief, tied in the middle. "Reckon how much is in here?" she asked as Earlene jerked it out of her hand.

"Never you mind how much money it is!" Earlene snapped as she untied the knot in the handkerchief.

"You reckon they might be enough to get me some skates or something, Ma?" Bertha went on and her face was all lit up with hope.

"They a-going to *steal* the money too!" Luther hissed like he couldn't believe that neither.

"I reckon they ain't nothing in the world so lowdown that them Hicksons wouldn't do it," I hissed back.

"Me and your pa will count out this change," Earlene answered Bertha. "And if they is enough here, it might be Santa Claus will have you a nice pair of skates under the Christmas tree come Christmas morning."

We watched old Bertha's face brighten up like the lights on the Christmas tree in the parlor. By then we heard the girls getting ready to come out of the kitchen and Earlene started tossing things back into the basket. "Pick up them ribbons and papers, Berthie!" she said as she jerked the basket from the table and thump-thumped out to the parlor as fast as she could go on them wide flat feet.

Bertha rushed around the table and bent down to the floor, grabbing up wrappings as quick as she could, then trotted off behind her ma.

"They ain't nothing but pure old thiefs!" Luther exclaimed like he still couldn't believe what he seen.

I left the doorway with a sick feeling inside me and Luther follered me. I headed straight back to the bedroom. Soon as I got there I put on my coat and yanked my bill cap out of the pocket and shoved it over my head.

"Where you going?" Jimmy asked, leaning around the doorway and peering into the room. Grady and Luther gathered round me, asking questions and watching me.

"I'm getting out of here!" I told Jimmy, and Grady and Luther looked surprised.

"But where are you going to go, Robert?" Jimmy asked. He come into the room then, looking up at me from his thin, sad face. His cheeks was still smudged from crying.

"I ain't going to live in this thieving old house no longer. No, sir. Not me. I'm going to find my ma," I answered with determination stinging at my voice.

"Aw, you ain't got no ma," Grady said, grinning and giving me a sideways look.

"You're just an orphan like us," Luther said, shoving his hands into his pockets and squinting his eyes at me.

"No, I ain't! I ain't no orphan! I been in foster homes, but I got a ma somewheres and I aim to find her!" I said it like I meant it and no one had better not say a word about it.

"You never said nothing about no ma," Luther went on.

"Well, fact of the matter is, I just only found out about her. And I'm heading out to find her."

"What if old Phineas finds out and stops you? You know you'd end up in the cellar for a solid week," Grady said.

"If you fellers keep quiet about what I told you, he won't never find me," I said as I headed toward the winder. No need to try and walk out the front door like a big shot, I decided. With my luck so far, old Phineas was bound to come home and head through the front door at the same time I was going out!

All the fellers follered me to the winder. I raised it, looped my foot over the sill, and looked back. Jimmy was about to cry again. His chin was trembling. "Aw . . ." I muttered from way down deep in my throat. Then I reached out and knocked on his dirty head with my knuckles, turned quickly, and sent my other leg over the sill and ran across the yard and out to the road. As I rushed across the road feeling the chill wind bite at me, I could hear the boys clamoring at the winder, trying to watch me. Their whispered goodbyes carried through the wind and I had to wipe at my nose for some reason. They ain't nothing so sad as whispers of goodbye drifting across a cold winter's night.

Chapter Six

I turned away from looking at the house just in time to see headlights coming down the road toward me. It was Phineas chugging along in his old car. I run as fast as I could, behind the Bower house, and stopped next to their henhouse. The chickens commenced to cluck and fly around. I looked back at the road. I could see Phineas turning the car into the yard of the house. After a minute he got out, slammed the door, and walked up to the front door, opened it and went inside.

It wouldn't be long and he'd know I was gone. Well, that was his little red wagon. I aimed to outrun him and outfox him and outdo him any way I could to get away from him. *If* he come after me, that is. Chances was he'd be glad I was gone, which suited me just fine.

After the door closed behind Phineas, I started walking up toward the hills that run behind the town. I still weren't sure just how I was going to get away. Maybe I'd walk my way out of town or maybe I'd hitch a ride with someone. I was thinking hard on it when I caught the sound of something not far from me. I stopped and looked around to the trees a little ways from me. Everything seemed still in the stripped, winter-blackened trees. I started walking again. But the sound come again, like someone running through the leaves and crushing them into the damp ground. I slowed my pace and perked my ears up. The noise repeated itself and I went cold all over. Phineas! He must not have gone into the house after all. It had to be him running up the hill behind me, just waiting to grab me! My heart commenced to pound. Next thing I knowed I heard my name called out in a low, urgent way. It were a girl's voice! I snapped around just in time to see a figure move out from behind one of the black trees. It were wearing a big old long flowing coat.

"All right, who are you?" I asked and my voice was trembling.

"It's me! Abiah!"

"What are you doing here? Get away from here! You want old Phineas to catch you out here with me?" I tried to keep my voice at a whisper, but it rose up high and shrill sounding.

"Don't worry, Robert. I'd run back to the home before I'd let him catch you," Abiah called out and she started running toward me with her old ragged coat flying out behind her. I recognized the coat as one some old lady who come to the home give her. It was miles too big and too long and it were ugly as all get out.

"How come you to foller me, Abiah?" I demanded when she reached me. I didn't want to sound mean, but I didn't want her with me, neither. No need for her to be punished if we was caught.

"I want to run away with you. Luther and Grady, they said you was running away to find your mama."

"I'm going to find my ma, all right, but you ain't going with me."

"Oh, *please*, Robert! I can't stay here no more! You got to let me go with you!" she pleaded.

"Well . . ." I commenced to think hard on it.

"*Please*, Robert! I won't be no trouble at all to you. I'll be like a little shadder, just follering you. I won't bother you ner nothing." I could hear the thickness in her throat and, even though I couldn't see her face good in the darkness, I knowed they was tears in her eyes.

I still wasn't too sure. "What you expect to do, dog my tracks from now on?"

"I just want to get away from here. If I can leave with you, it'll be a start."

"Well . . . all right, then," I said grudgingly. I sure hadn't counted on taking no one with me. "But you got to leave off somewheres along the way. I'm on my way to Mill Springs and you can't go there with me. That's where my ma is."

"How you know your ma wants to be with you, Robert?" she asked and we started walking, climbing the hill slowly.

"I just know, that's all."

"And how do you know she's in that place, in that Mill Springs you mentioned?"

"I heard Reverend Shamlin tell old Earlene when I was sent down to the cellar. He said he knowed my ma and told Earlene where she was." We panted to the top of the hill and started down the other side to where the railroad tracks run. In the darkness we could see the huge outline of the boxcars parked on the tracks. I stopped and turned to Abiah, trying to see her face. "If old Phineas come looking for me and found just you, would you tell him where I was?" I asked it, just to see if I could trust her.

"Not even if he tied me to a tree and threatened to hammer nails through my head!" she answered, looking right up into my face.

"You sure?"

"And not even if he poked both my eyes out!"

"Aw . . ." I turned my head and give a little laugh.

"It's true! And not even if he cut off all my fingers and I couldn't pick up a thing!"

"What would you do if he chased you?"

"I'd jump up to the sky and hide behind the stars!"

I had to laugh a little more. It took a girl to talk like that.

"Well, sounds like I could trust you a little," I said.

"You can trust me *a lot,* Robert." They was such a pure sound of honesty in Abiah's voice that I decided I *could* trust her a lot.

"You got to keep up with me if you expect to go with me," I told her. "I'm going to be in Mill Springs by Christmas day and you got to go on by yourself." I frowned hard at her then. "You do got somewhere you want to go, don't you?"

"Oh, sure. Sure I do," she answered real quick. Then she asked, "How come you want to be in Mill Springs by Christmas day?"

"I'm going to be my ma's Christmas present," I told her.

We reached the railroad tracks where a big freight train with a long line of boxcars was stopped dead still on the tracks. Some of them boxcars carried fruits and vegetables and even cattle, clear across the country sometimes. And sometimes the boxcars was vacant, like they was waiting for the hobos who walked along the tracks to hitch a ride in them. Sometimes, when we was finished with chores at the Hicksons', me and Grady would climb the hill and watch the trains go by, huffing and puffing and blowing out smoke and steam, and at night we could hear the long, low whistle they give out as they rushed by. All at once it come to me how we was going to get out of town.

"You ever ride the rails?" I asked Abiah, turning to look at her darkened profile as she stared at the train.

"Nope," she answered.

"Well, I reckon there's a first time for everything," I said and reached for her hand. It was small and bony and cold, and I felt like if I pressed too hard I might break her little fingers right in my hand.

We run to the tracks and I struggled a minute to get up into the boxcar. It was high up off the tracks and I couldn't make it in one try. When I finally did, I leaned down to pull Abiah up into the darkness with me. Once inside, we commenced to try and get the big sliding door closed, but we could only budge it a little way, it was so heavy. We stopped and looked around. It was so dark we couldn't see a thing. Suddenly we felt the train jerk and heard the screech of the huge wheels on the track as it started to move. We swayed against each other and trembled with the sudden vibration of the movement. We heard the chug and puff of the engine as the train picked up speed, felt the rush of wind curling through the boxcar, and heard the wail of the whistle that fell across the night and over the hills of the town.

I felt for Abiah's hand again. "Are you scared?" I asked with my heart pounding.

"Not much," she answered but I could hear her voice shake.

I squeezed her hand and took in a deep breath. I was on my way, headed for Mill Springs, I hoped, and my ma.

Chapter Seven

We searched until we found the wall of the boxcar, sat down, and leaned against it. We could feel the vibration of the wheels as the train rocked and swayed along the tracks and we could smell the odd odor of the wind whipping around inside the car and the cold way it felt pushing against our necks and hair. After a while Abiah said, "How you know we're headed toward Mill Springs, Robert?"

"I don't. Alls I can do is hope. I'll find out soon as we stop somewhere near a town."

I heard her shiver then she said, "It's almost as cold in here as it is outside."

"Boxcars wasn't meant to haul humans, I reckon."

"Well, it's better than being in that mean old home with Bertha. Just about anyplace is better than that." I agreed even though I'd been in even worse homes. Then I asked her where she aimed to go when she left me. "Well . . . I ain't exactly decided yet," she answered and it sure did sound uncertain to me.

"I thought you had a place in mind. Someone you knowed of you could go to," I said sharply.

"No . . . well, maybe I do."

"*Maybe?* You *got* to have, Abiah. You can't go to my ma's with me! I'm going alone."

"I didn't say I was, did I?" she flared up real quick. Then, changing the subject, her voice got real soft when she said, "I always wished I had a winder seat with red velvet cushions I could set on and look out into a pretty yard all filled with flowers. I always wished, ever since I been in them nasty homes, that I could see my daddy and mama coming up to the front door, smiling at me through the winder. I can close my eyes, Robert, and see just how it ought to be. I can see it in my mind as big as you please."

I frowned through the darkness, trying to see Abiah's face. I could only imagine her sad eyes and her short, cut-off, stringy hair plastered down over her forehead and the sides of her face, the way it always seemed to be.

"I think real hard all the time," she went on. "But their faces won't come. There's just a man and a woman coming to the front door of the house and I can't even remember what they looked like. I can't remember my little sister neither. But I know I had one. Seems like when I try to, she always turns into a doll. Just a doll that don't move, just sets and stares. I don't even know who I look like, do you, Robert? You reckon you look like your ma and pa?"

I had to think on that. I had dark hair and dark eyes, and a regular build, just like any feller my age. They wasn't nothing extry special about me, but I hoped I did favor them in some way. "I don't know," I said finally.

"You reckon you'll really find your ma?"

"Yes," I said with all the determination I had inside me.

"And will it really be Christmas day, you reckon?"

"That's what I'm aiming for."

"How many days till then?"

"Eleven. I counted off the days on Phineas's calendar he had on the wall behind his desk."

The train jerked and pulled and tilted and the wind seemed to whip even harder through the wide-open door. "I sure am hungry," I said after a minute and I rubbed my hand in a circle around my belly. I felt like I hadn't et in a long, long time.

"I brought some food," Abiah said brightly.

"You did? What did you bring?" I asked excitedly and I could feel her digging down in her coat pocket.

"It's just some corn bread, but it's sweet corn bread. I took it out of the kitchen. I didn't have no time to get nothing else. Put your hand out."

I stretched out my hand and she dropped a crumbly piece of corn bread into it. I took a bite and it was as dry as sawdust. I chewed it up and swallered it anyway, but when I started to put another bite in my mouth a sudden, bright light exploded like a flash of lightning in my face and the corn bread, what was left of it, was jerked out of my hand. Abiah gave out with a sharp, frightened yell and fell against me. We was both trembling like hell's own fury as we looked up into the face behind a lit match. It was wrinkled and ugly, and gray hair hung down along the ears. The grin on the whiskery face was as cruel as old Bertha's was.

"So! You got food, huh!" The man bellered out from a deep,

gravelly-sounding voice and he shoved my corn bread into his mouth and chewed fast and hard, like he was starved to death almost. The corn bread fell out the sides of his mouth as he chewed. "Got anything else?" he asked gruffly. We shook our heads and Abiah tried to move even closer to me. "You'd best not be telling me no lie," he warned and we shook our heads.

"Going to Mill Springs, huh," he said and he chuckled huskily, then wiped his mouth with the back of his hand. "Oh, I heard you. Been layin' not an inch away, taking in every word. Runnin' away, too, huh." He chuckled again and the match flame wavered from the force of his breath.

Neither one of us answered. The man looked from each of our faces and suddenly the match went out. He quickly struck another one against the leg of his pants and peered into our faces again. "Where'd you come from, anyway?" We was too scared to make a peep. "Well, you don't have to tell me nothin'. I'm runnin' away too. I'm runnin' from the laws." He laughed real hard and I could feel Abiah tremble against me.

My fear turned to terror and cut a sharp path all the way through me. The laws! No telling what he'd done! I squeezed Abiah's hand and she squeezed mine back.

"I been ridin' the rails for a mighty long time, keepin' ahead of them. They think they'll catch me one day. But they won't. I'm too slick for them. I'm as slick as a snake in the grass! You hear what I said?" He leaned clear down to stare into our faces. We couldn't see him good in the darkness, but his breath was against our cheeks, smelling of stale tobaccer and the sweet corn bread.

"Y–yes, s–sir," me and Abiah managed to mutter.

"Sir! I ain't been called 'sir' since . . . well, no matter. I'm gettin' off when this here train goes around the bend. Anybody asks you anything, you ain't seen hide ner hair of me. You hear?" His face come close to ours again and we pulled back, "We–we understand," I spoke up. "We ain't looking for no trouble."

"You're a smart kid," he said and he moved back from us.

"Sir, one thing!" I said real quick. "Could you tell me, is this train headed in the direction of Mill Springs?"

"Change cars in Alberta Falls," he barked and all at once he was in the door of the boxcar, his outline brightened by the moon.

The train slowed and the wheels squealed on the tracks, chugged and rattled, and started to pull slow and hard, going around the bend. It moved like a cautious worm along the tracks, shuddering and wobbling and almost stopping. In that instant the man leaped from the door of the boxcar. Me and Abiah scrambled up, teetering and rocking against the wall and, holding on to each other, we made it to the door. Nothing but the wind and the brightness of the moon, millions of shadders and black trees, hills and distant houses and farms, met our eyes. The man was gone.

We stood in the doorway with the cold wind blowing over us as the train finished the turn and moved out straight on the tracks again. It picked up speed and the wheels clattered and screeched, pounding against the tracks like thundering horses. We made it back to the wall and sunk to the floor.

"You reckon they is anyone else in here with us?" Abiah whispered jerkily, close to my ear.

"I–I c–can't say," I whispered back.

We sat quiet and still for a long time, listening and waiting for some sound or movement to come from inside the boxcar, but none come and pretty soon we commenced to talk normal again. But our talk kept turning to food. We kept wishing the man hadn't stole the corn bread.

"What you reckon the laws is after that feller for, Robert?"

"Maybe he killed someone. I don't know. You never know who you'll meet up with when you ride the rails," I said like I knowed all about it.

"I reckon we was lucky he only took our corn bread," Abiah said and yawned.

"You can't go to sleep! We got to stay awake for when we get to Alberta Falls and can get off," I told her.

"You ever been to Alberta Falls?"

"Yeah. I lived there with a family once. It's a bigger place than Temple is. Lots of trains go through there."

"If we went to see that family you lived with, you reckon they would give us some food?"

"They wouldn't give me the directions into hell even if they didn' hate me!" I answered in disgust. That family was just as bad as all the others I'd lived with. I didn't have no special need to see them ever again.

Seemed like the hum and jounce of the train made us sleep a little after all. But soon as I felt it slow down, I sat up straight and alert. Lights flashed past the door of the boxcar and the train moved even slower. I stood up and peered out. The moon was gone and daylight had come. A damp, foggy mist fell over everything. Alberta Falls! We was pulling into the switching yard, surrounded by tracks filled with other cars. Down on the ground I could see brakemen out in the fog all bundled up in heavy jackets and wearing striped overalls and bill caps, walking around.

"Abiah!" I called and she jumped and opened her eyes. "I think they're going to take this car off and put another one on. We got to get off now."

"What do you mean?" she asked sleepily.

"I mean we got to jump off before they start switching cars. We could end up back in Temple if we don't." We could already hear the grating, jarring creak of cars being switched onto other tracks and the voices of the railmen calling out to each other. "Come on! Hurry!" I said. Abiah leaped up and rushed to the door. I grabbed her hand but she hung back, looking scared. "Come on! You got to jump!" I told her impatiently.

"I'm afraid to! I never jump off of nothing!" she protested, but I didn't have time for that! I yanked her hand hard against all her grumbling and protesting and pulled her with me when I swooped out the boxcar door.

We landed in hard, damp dirt at the edge of an embankment. Lucky for us the train was on tracks on the outside of the others and it was likely no one seen us. All around us was noise and activity, the switching of the cars on the tracks, the sound of train whistles, trains pulling into the station, trains pulling out, voices rising out of the fog shouting orders and in the distance a conductor's voice calling out, "Shelby . . . All aboard for Shelby!"

"You okay, Abiah?" I asked, pulling her up from the ground.

She coughed and grumbled a sharp, "I reckon!" and pulled the big old baggy coat tightly around her. She looked all lost in it when it was pulled around her like that, like a little turtle in a big shell with only its head sticking out. Her hair was in her face, all stringy and loose like it hadn't never seen a comb. Looking at her, I reached up with both hands and smoothed my own hair back.

We lurked at the edge of the boxcar, peering all around, watching the brakemen walking along the tracks, praying they wouldn't catch us. No telling what they would do if they knowed we rid the train free! Pretty soon we seen men of all shapes and sizes, wearing wrinkled clothes and old hats, pile cautiously out of some of the boxcars. Just like us they lurked, silently watching the brakemen and, when they seen their chance, they took off, scattering in all directions, skittering off along the tracks between the cars.

Soon as the way seemed clear, me and Abiah run too, leaping across the tracks and between the big steel cars as fast as we could go. At the end of one of the cars where we waited, we seen a lone man hurrying in our direction. He looked like all them other men who had jumped out of the boxcars and run. When he got close, we could see his sleepy-looking, bloodshot eyes and the whiskers that growed like a patch of weeds around his face. His clothes was so dirty, they looked like they could stand alone without any help from him.

I kept a watchful eye on him and when he reached us he slowed his walk and stared, then said a tired-sounding, "Morning," nodded his head, and started to go on by. I reckoned from his greeting it was safe to speak to him.

"Sir, could you tell me when the next freight pulls out of here heading north?"

"They got two that I know about. One's around six in the evening and the other one is way late, one or two o'clock in the morning. How come you to ask?" He stopped and give me a curious eye then, like he was wondering how come a kid to be hanging around the railroad tracks asking such a question. I thought about Phineas and if he might of got the laws on us and decided not to ask too much.

"Oh . . . er . . . well, I just was wondering is all," I answered. Then real fast I asked, "You know if that freight going north is headed toward Mill Springs?"

"Headed that way, but a feller would have to make a change in Marketville," he answered, then he looked at Abiah and studied her real hard. "I got a daughter back in Tennessee about your age. She's with her mama."

"How come you ain't with them?" Abiah asked.

"No work in my town no more. Man's got to support his family or he's got to leave, find work where he can. He ain't much of a man if he don't," he said and abruptly walked on. After a second or two, like a train, he picked up speed in his walk and the next thing he was running fast and had latched on to a moving freight and disappeared into the wide-open door of a boxcar.

"Well," I said, "it looks like we got a long time to wait till six o'clock." We seen the coast was clear and started running. The dampness sent a deep chill through us, but even that didn't feel so bad after being cooped up in that boxcar all that time.

After a little, we was close enough to the train depot to see people gathered up near the tracks with their satchels and boxes and others flowing out over the platform, going into the station. We hurried through the crowd and around to the back of the station, into the shadows. We was getting more and more hungry, but after living at the Hicksons' and always being shorted on the food the way we was, it weren't like we was some rich kids used to steady meals and heaping plates.

Behind the building we stopped and turned to stare through the winder where a small, scraggly Christmas tree sat on a table decorated with very old, worn-out-looking ornaments. I reckoned it was put there for the pleasure of the travelers.

"Oh! Ain't it pretty!" Abiah cried as she put her nose up against the winder glass and stared at it.

"Nothing like the Hicksons'. That was the grandest Christmas tree I ever seen in my whole life. Just like the one I'm going to get for me and my ma when I get to Mill Springs," I bragged.

Abiah turned from the winder and looked at me. "You think you'll make it to Mill Springs on Christmas day, Robert? You really think you will?" There was a sound of dread in her voice. I looked at her face. It was dirty and tinged pink from the cold.

"When that freight pulls out of here at six o'clock, I aim to be on it. I'll get there all right."

Abiah's face crumpled. "What you going to do about me?"

"Ain't you got someplace you wanted to go? Weren't that the deal between us?" I asked, frowning over her.

"What if . . . what if I *ain't* got no place to go?" she asked and her eyes was all sad and her face was sad and it made me feel sad just to look at her with her old, windy, knotted hair piled up like a tumbleweed on her head and smudges on her cheeks.

"Well . . . we got to find you a place," I said and before she could make a protest, an old, mangy-looking black dog that looked all rib bones and hanging tongue come loping up to us and started licking Abiah's hand.

"Get away, mutt," I said, but the dog wouldn't get away.

"Leave him stay," Abiah said and she scratched at the dog's head with the hand it had licked.

"We got to go and find something to eat," I told her and I pulled her hand and made her run, but the dog run too and wouldn't stop except when we stopped. I told it to get away again. But it wouldn't. All it done was stop and look at me like it was as big an orphan as me and Abiah was. We started running again and the dog took off with us. As skinny and bony as it was, I couldn't see how it had enough energy to run. But maybe he was running away from someplace, too, I thought.

"Might as well let him come along. He aims to anyway," Abiah said breathlessly as we ran.

"I reckon you're right," I agreed and I didn't have to look back to see the old dog. He was traveling right along with us, yapping and panting at my side with his tongue hanging out.

Chapter Eight

Hey! Where you kids running to?" someone called out, and me and Abiah looked at each other.

"Don't stop!" I cautioned her and I speeded up my run, dragging her along with that old coat she had on flying like a big tent behind her. The mutt dog was right there at our heels, running like a son-of a-gun.

"Hey! I said. Where you kids running to?" The voice come again and I commenced to tremble all over. I was half out of breath too. "I got a whole box of mistletoe here to sell! Help me sell it and I'll give you two cents apiece on it!"

"Did you hear that?" Abiah said and her voice shook through her breath.

We stopped running and turned around. An old man in a wool scarf and cap stood beside a building with a sign on it that read, CREAMERY. They was a striped awning over a front winder and signs that told the prices of ice cream and all the different flavors. They was drawings on the signs, too, of bowls with scoops of ice cream in them.

We had run into the business part of town. Stores looked like they had been open awhile and people was swarming in and out of them. The fog lifted but it was still cold and overcast.

"You say two cents apiece, mister?" I called out to the old man.

"That's right," he called back. "Come on over here and get some. You can work right around on this street. Lots of Christmas shoppers here."

Me and Abiah looked at each other and sort of nodded our heads in agreement. Two cents added up to whatever we sold might buy us something to eat, I thought. When we got to the old man, he leaned down to the box that sat on the sidewalk beside his feet and pulled out a big handful of mistletoe tied together in little bunches.

"Here," he said, "this ought to do the both of you for a while. Ask for five cents. Folks'll pay it. It's Christmas and there ain't a lad or lassie won't pay that just to get a kiss under it." The old man threw his head back and laughed at what he said. Me and Abiah exchanged another look.

We split the mistletoe up between us and the old man pointed in the direction he wanted us to go. "Stay on the main street. That's where the shoppers with money is," he told us.

"Yes, sir," I told him and we started walking off with the old mutt dog trotting right beside us.

We passed shop after shop where toys and bright decorations and pretty clothes hung in the winders. In lots of the shops they was even Christmas trees all lit up in the winders and big green wreaths with bows on them hanging on the front doors. Shoppers was going in and out carrying packages. We stopped before a toy store where they seemed to be plenty of activity.

"You stay here by this door and I'll go on down to the next store," I told Abiah. Then I looked at the old mutt. "You stay here with her!" I added. The old mutt looked at me like he didn't want to, but he moved over closer to Abiah and sat down on his tail, his big eyes still watching me.

"Wanna buy some mistletoe, mister?" I heard Abiah ask someone as I walked away. "You hold it over your girlfriend's head and she'll give you a big smacker!"

"I don't have a girlfriend, young lady! I have a wife!" the man snapped impatiently and went hurrying off down the street. That didn't seem to bother Abiah. "You wanna buy some mistletoe, ma'am? You put it over your old man's head and he'll give you a big old smacker," she repeated to the next person to come out of the shop.

"Why, I just might at that. How much is it?" the lady asked in a friendly way.

"Only five cents, ma'am," Abiah told her.

"Five cents?" the woman asked.

"Yes, ma'am," Abiah answered and the woman dug down in her purse and pulled out a coin and give it to her.

"Let me have two bunches of that mistletoe, dear," the woman said and I bugged out my eyes. Looked to me like Abiah was going to do all right.

I stopped in front of a toy shop where people was going in and out the door all loaded down with packages. "Sir," I said to the first gent who come out the door, "would you be interested in some mistletoe for Christmas? It's only just five cents," I said as polite as I knowed how.

The man stopped and reached into his pocket. "Here, son," he said and he handed me a nickel. I held the mistletoe out to him, but he rushed away saying, "Forget it. Keep the nickel and sell it to someone else."

I bugged my eyes again. It sure was a surprise how folks was acting. It weren't no time and all that mistletoe was gone and sold. We was right pleased with ourselves and so hungry our bellies was talking to us, telling us to send down some food! When we got back together, we started counting out the money we'd made, walking along and talking about what we was going to get to eat with our share.

"Since I always been so shorted on pertaters, I'm going to go right into a cafe and tell them alls I want to eat is a big plate of pertaters with lots of butter on it," I told Abiah and she laughed and punched my arm.

"I'm going to get me some eggs and bacon. Maybe I'll even have enough money to get two orders," Abiah said.

"You'll be lucky to get even *one* order. We ain't earned *that* much money," I told her.

We was talking in this way and making up all the things we was going to eat when we seen two big fellers walking toward us. They looked so mean hell wouldn't have them. They come swaggering up to us with their chins pushed out and a threatening look in their eyes. "What'cha got there?" the one wearing a plaid jacket and a knit cap asked and he folded his arms over his chest and stared at us.

"Ain't got nothing," I answered and started to poke the change I made into my pocket. Abiah moved close to me.

"Ain't got nothing, huh?" the other kid asked like he knowed I was lying, and all of a sudden he grabbed my hand and pulled it out and the next thing I knowed, the kid in the plaid jacket was doing the same thing to Abiah and, before we could get our wits about us, our coins was tore out of our hands and them mean, ornery fellers was beating it off down the street.

"Sic 'um!" I shouted at the mutt dog, pointing my arm in the direction the boys run. But that carnsarn old fleabitten dog wouldn't budge. "Go after them guys, I told you!" I shouted again, but that dumb dog just stared at me with his tail flapping against the sidewalk. I scrunched up my face and jutted my chin out and told him, "If you don't go after them guys, you ain't going a step more with us!"

He seemed to understand that, and the second I said it, his ears shot up along with his tail and he went ripping down the street, barking after them fellers like they was being chewed alive. Soon the mutt come flying back with a piece of shirt hanging out of his mouth and panting to beat sixty.

"Good thing you done that," I told him as I pulled the piece of cloth out of his mouth and tossed it to the ground. I patted his head to let him know he done good even though he couldn't bring back the money.

Abiah sighed deeply and shoved her hands down into the pockets of that old baggy coat. "Well, what we going to do now?" she asked downheartedly.

"Durn it! Durn it! Durn it!" I exploded, pounding my fists into my leg. Didn't do no good though. The money was gone. "Well," I said finally, "might as well go on back to the old man, tell him what happened, and ask him if he's got any more mistletoe we can sell."

We started walking off and the mutt dog was beside me like he thought he was my best friend. But the truth was I weren't all that crazy about him. When we got close to the creamery building, the old man seen us coming and cracked a big smile. He greeted us with pats on our backs, saying, "Well, you sold all the mistletoe! Good. Now, where's the money and we'll settle up."

"The money was tooken from us," Abiah spoke up and the smile on the old man's face faded into a grim, accusing scowl.

"What do you mean, took from you?" he demanded in a loud, angry voice. Mutt Dog commenced to sniff around the old man's trousers.

"Two fellers, big and mean as all get-out, come up to us and took it right out of our hands," I said. "Wasn't nothing we could do about it, sir."

The old man muttered something and kicked at Mutt Dog. "They had faces as mean looking as you look right now," Abiah spoke up and suddenly the old man raised back his hand and struck her right across her ear. "Damned little liars!" he raged and his face was full of disgust and hatred. "I'll teach you to sell my mistletoe and keep the money!" He lunged at me then, but I dodged and he didn't get a lick in. "Police! Police!" he started yelling to the top of his lungs and people from up and down the street and from around corners and stepping out of stores commenced to swarm toward us.

I grabbed Abiah's hand and started pulling. As we made a beeline down the street, she was holding her other hand over her ear that the old man boxed, moaning and half crying, and Mutt Dog was running ahead of us, his floppy ears jumping and bouncing on his head. We made it all the way down the street, weaving in and out of the crowd, flying past the shops, crossed over the street, and beat it around a corner where no one was walking and only a few cars was passing up and down. We raced to the first building we seen and crouched down against the wall behind some bushes. The wind had turned bitter, and a draft was going right down my neck. We could still hear the old man shouting for the police.

Chapter Nine

As we leaned against the building we could hear the faint sound of an organ and singing voices coming through the wall. I looked up at the winder just above us and seen it had stained glass of all colors in it.

"It's a church, Abiah," I said. But they weren't no time to dwell on it. No telling if the laws was coming after us or not. I looked down at Abiah. "You all right?" I asked her.

"My ear hurts," she answered in a tiny whimper. Her hand was still covering it.

"That's what we get for trying to help that old geezer and ourselves, too," I told her and I was filled with bitterness at what happened.

Mutt Dog moved in real close to Abiah and licked the hand she held over her ear. She put her hand down and scratched at his neck. Then he licked his tongue over her ear just like he knowed she was in pain and wanted to comfort her. She laughed and I reckon it made her feel better. I scrunched over close to her and pulled the collar of her old coat up close around her neck to keep the wind off her ear.

"I'm sorry, Abiah," I said as gently as I knowed how. "I'm awful sorry you got your ears boxed."

"It weren't your fault, Robert," she said and blinked her eyes at me. She looked awful pretty, even with her dirty face and her tumbleweed hair and it seemed like all of a sudden I wanted to protect her.

I cleared my throat, for I was about to say something important to her. "Abiah," I said, "I reckon you and me had better stick together after all."

Her eyes grew wide. "You mean I can go on with you to Mill Springs where your ma is?"

"My ma, she could see about your ear and take care of you. Make you some dresses maybe," I said. I sure had changed my mind quick!

Abiah smiled, looking pleased and happy. "Seems like my ear don't hurt half so bad since you told me that, Robert."

I looked around at the street in the direction we'd run from. Cars was still moving up and down it, but I didn't see no extry activity. Maybe the laws had gone in a different direction. But it was best not to take chances, to get off the street just in case. The day was moving on and the glow from the lights in the church winder looked warm and cozy. The music poured out with such sweetness it made my heart feel lonesome to see my ma. I thought about her and how much further I had to go to get to her and how proud I was going to be to see her at last. It all made a lump come to my throat.

"Let's go inside," I told Abiah and my voice was all thick. It would be warm inside the church and we could sit down in the back near the door and listen to the hymns.

We got up and started up the church steps and old Mutt Dog come jumping up the steps with us.

"No," I said to him. "You got to stay here." He sat down at the top of the steps like he didn't like it a bit.

I pushed the heavy door open a little and peered inside. Warm air rushed out at me and made my skin tingle. The seats was filled up in front where the choir was singing, but most of the back ones, close to the door, was empty. I took Abiah's hand and we stepped through the door and moved as quietly as we could into the far corner of one of the rows, near the wall. We no sooner got set down when Mutt Dog commenced whining and scratching at the door.

"Durned old pest of a dog!" I muttered to Abiah. She leaned her head back against the seat and breathed a deep, forlorn-sounding sigh.

I looked around the church. Folks was dressed right well, with hats and gloves and good coats and the choir wore dark robes and sung so beautiful that their voices rose all the way up to the rafters and fell back down again like a soft rain. I leaned my head back and started to get comfortable in the warmth of the room and the warmth of the singing.

I'd just started to close my eyes when I seen a face that looked familiar. I stared hard. Up front, in the choir, with his mouth wide open, singing like a pure Christian, was that mean, ornery feller that stole the mistletoe money from me and Abiah! Standing next to him was his sidekick! They looked like the cleanest-living boys you'd ever want to meet, like to steal would of been the last thing they would ever think about doing. Well, I thought, it just proves what I already knowed. You can't trust no one. Not even church boys singing in a choir!

I punched Abiah's arm. But she had already seen them. "We'd better go," I whispered, leaning close to her.

"Let's wait a minute. They ain't doing nothing but singing and it's warm in here," she said and I wrinkled my brow at her.

We set there a minute or two more with me getting more jittery by the second. Finally I punched Abiah's arm again, but she wouldn't budge. She was as bad as old Mutt Dog!

Next thing we knowed, the service was over and folks was starting to stand up and the choir was breaking apart. Them fellers spotted us right off as they started down the aisle. They was headed in our direction, not taking their eyes off us. I reckoned they hadn't forgot how Mutt Dog had chased them and tore off a piece of one of their shirts.

I yanked Abiah up from the seat and we hightailed it out the door and down the front steps so fast we almost tripped and fell over Mutt Dog, still waiting outside the door.

"Run!" I shouted at Abiah as I jerked her along the street by her hand.

"STOP! You're the ones that sicked that mangy dog on us! Stop!" we heard one of them fellers yell out and we could hear their heels clipping along behind us.

We run so fast and so far that it seemed everything we passed was nothing but one long stringy blur. After a while the clipping noise behind us stopped and all we could hear was our own feet on the ground and old Mutt Dog rasping for breath beside us. Finally we was so out of breath ourselves that we had to stop and fall to the ground. Seemed like it was a long time before we could get our breath back, and when we did, we seen that we had fell to the ground near an old, moss-covered stone wall that had lots of the stones missing out of it. Across the wall and over a little meadow was a house all strung out with Christmas tree lights at the winders.

"What's wrong?" Abiah asked after she got her breath. "Why are you looking like that?"

I pulled my eyes away from the house and looked at Abiah. "I know this place," I told her. "It's the Eldon place. I used to live here."

"You mean it's that foster home you stayed in?" she asked and she got up on her knees and peered through one of the spaces where a stone was missing.

"Yeah," I answered. I hated the place more than a hog loves mud. I hated them Eldons too and all the bad memories I had of living there. Fact was, it was even worse than old Phineas and Earlene's place was, if that could be possible.

Old man Eldon believed in fresh air for everyone except his own self! In winter he'd leave the whole house cold, all the fires out, and us kids would near about freeze. But if you passed the old man's door at night, you could feel the heat from his fireplace in the bedroom. You could tell he was nice and cozy-warm in that room while all us kids was hanging around with our hands in our pockets and our teeth chattering.

After I told Abiah some things about the place she asked, "How come him to do that, Robert?"

"How come a lamb to have wool?" I asked with a snort. "I reckon the old codger was born that way. Mean. Just like all the rest of them foster home people is."

Abiah huddled deep into her old coat. It had drug the ground for so long, through spit and everything else it had picked up, that it weren't fit to wear. "They got some good homes, Robert. I was in one once. I even had my own bed and a quilt the old mama had made herself. But the old papa got sick and died and I had to go to another home. It sure was nice in that home. All warm and sweet."

"Well," I said grudgingly, "they ain't many around like that one. Leastways none that I seen."

"Ain't they never been no one good to you?"

I thought for a minute. "They was a feller lived in the Eldons' home. His name was Dewey. We was right good friends. But that was a long time ago," I told her and I clipped it right off.

Old Mutt Dog whined and looked at both of us like he was wondering what we was going to do next.

"If we keep going to Mill Springs, we'll need warm coats," I said as I watched Abiah tremble and shiver in that rag of a coat. "I bet old man Eldon wouldn't even miss a coat or two if we was to take them."

"What are you talking about?" Abiah asked, frowning at me.

"I know exactly how to get into that house and where all the coats is kept. Oh, I wouldn't take none that belonged to no orphan kid. I'd take the best and newest-looking ones because the best and newest-looking ones would belong to the Eldon family, probably bought with money from the county, meant for the kids." I said it with bitterness.

"You going to do it, Robert? You really aiming to *steal* coats?" Abiah asked and she had a wide look of disbelief on her face.

"I reckon I am. Wait here," I told her and I hiked my foot up on the stone wall. Old Mutt tried to jump on the wall, but I pushed him back with my foot.

Abiah stood up. "I'm going too," she said.

"No!"

"You can't stop me, Robert!"

I looked down into what I could see of her face. It was darker now, but I could still see the determined expression she had. "Well, okay," I said finally and I leaned down and took her hand and pulled her over the stone wall with me.

Old Mutt leaped over the wall and trailed at our heels with his ears flying.

Chapter Ten

Even though it had been a few years since I'd been at the Eldons' place, I recognized everything from the huge old squeaking doors to the dark, ugly furniture in the front room to the tattered rugs and faded wallpaper. Even the pictures on the walls, the old grandfather clock that chimed every hour and on the half hour, and the raggedy-looking shawl that old man Eldon used to throw over his shoulders when he sat in the front room was still tossed across the back of his rocking chair. The smell of that place was the same too. Home-baked bread and carbolic acid! Me and some of the other boys used to go from door to door selling it in little tin cans. I reckoned from the smell, the Eldons still had a good supply on hand.

I even recognized the face that peered around the corner of the kitchen door soon as me and Abiah went through the winder.

"Dewey . . ." I said under my breath and the big smiling mouth opened into an even bigger one. It were Dewey, all right. Only his face was all changed from the big round ball it used to be into a narrow one with sunk-in cheeks and dark circles under the little gray eyes.

"Why . . . Bob!" he said and he moved away from the door and come toward me, coughing a little.

"My name is *Robert,*" I said right off. "It's all I got to call my own." I glanced at Abiah when I said it. I'd learned it from her, how important a name is when a person don't have nothing else.

Dewey's smile didn't fade. He stuck out his hand when he reached me and I shook it. "What'cha doin' here, B–Robert? I ain't seen you in so long. You come back here to live?"

"Hell, no!" I said like a toughie. "I'm on my way to Mill Springs to find my ma."

"Your ma? I didn't know you had a ma, B–Robert." Dewey coughed a little again.

"Why, sure, I got one. Me and Abiah here, we're going to live with her. Ain't we, Abiah?" I glanced at Abiah. She looked scared and only nodded her head.

"You don't say?" Dewey said, looking puzzled. I reckon he was remembering the times when I said I didn't have no ma ner pa. "Well, what'cha doing back at this old place?" he went on.

"I come to steal some coats," I said straight out and Dewey chuckled.

"Hell, I'll help you," he said, sounding as tough as me. "Which ones you want?" he asked as he headed off to the cloakroom, where all the old, ratty-smelling coats that was for the orphans laid in a pile in a corner of the floor. Me and Abiah follered him.

About that time old Mutt Dog commenced to whine out by the door where we left him. "You got a dog with you?" Dewey asked.

"Aw, just some old mutt that took a notion to foller us. Don't worry, he'll get wore out and go on when he sees we ain't going to open the door," I told him.

"Which ones do you want?" Dewey asked as soon as we entered the small, dim room with the high ceiling and light that hung down from the center of it. He rushed eagerly to the pile of old coats on the floor. They was all musty smelling and wrinkled looking. I got a sick feeling just to look at them and remember how all us kids had to pull coats out of the pile to wear in the winter. Things hadn't changed much around there at all.

"None of them," I told him and he stopped going through the coats and watched me as I turned to the coats that hung on hooks on the wall. They was almost new looking with bright colors and no bad smells about them. They belonged to the Eldon family. I studied them with a critical eye and Dewey said, "Oh, them," and he come over to where I stood and pulled down a dark wool jacket and looked at it. "This one here would fit you real good, B–Robert," and he coughed harder and longer this time.

"Don't you reckon you guys ought to be quiet?" Abiah asked in a hushed voice as she come up to us and started looking at the coats.

"Don't matter none," Dewey told her brightly. "Old man Eldon is deef as a dead rabbit. Can't hardly see ner talk a bit, neither. He had him a fine good fit a year ago and near about died. The old lady, she tooken the other kids off to a church feed. They're having a program too. A play and singing and such."

"How come you not to go?" I asked.

"I got to watch the old man. Always do."

Just then the grandfather clock struck five times. I chalked up the count in my mind.

"How come you not to plain-out hate that old fool, Dewey?" I asked, thinking back on the times old man Eldon cussed Dewey and pushed him around.

"Sure I hate the old devil! I stand behind him all the time and scream in his old hairy ears just how much I hate him. But he don't hear a word," Dewey said with a grin.

"You're a card, Dewey. You always was," I said and turned to look as Abiah pulled a coat off one of the hooks.

"This one!" she said and I seen her eyes all big and bright with the joy of looking at the coat. "This one! Can I have it?" The coat was a red one that was a little dirty in front, but looked soft and warm, too.

"Why, sure you can. It's the old lady's, but she don't never wear it much. She says red makes the old devil hisself come out in her and it sure does do that, all right. Try it on," Dewey urged Abiah and she shed her ugly long coat, let it fall to the floor, and quickly pulled on the red one.

When she had the coat on she looked different, like she had come alive. Her whole face looked brighter. She snuggled her chin into the collar and run her hands up and down the soft wool. Then she looked up and said, "Ain't it beautiful, Robert?"

"Looks like a good fit too," I said. It was about the right length and not too big. It sure put that old tent she'd been wearing to shame!

"I'm proud to let you have it," Dewey said with a wide smile, just like he owned it.

I pulled on the jacket. The sleeves was too long, but I folded them back and made them to fit. "I'll take this one," I told Dewey, like as if I was buying it. And just to be funny I added, "You don't have to wrap it up."

Soon as we finished fooling around with the coats, Abiah tugged on my sleeve and whispered, "I'm hungry, Robert. Ain't you?"

I turned to Dewey. "Dewey," I said, "me and Abiah ain't et in a long while. You reckon you could show us some kitchen hospitality?"

"Why, sure. Come on," he said like he was the head of the house.

As we follered him into the kitchen, he bent forward and coughed a few times real hard. Me and Abiah looked at each other and frowned. Dewey sure was coughing a lot.

The kitchen was the same old ugly place I remembered, with its big dirty table filled with bread crumbs and grease spots, old rattletrap chairs, a dark, flyspecked shade at the winder, and a dim light that hung down from the ceiling. Dewey pulled a slab of homemade bread from a box on the messy counter and cut us off big chunks. Then he spread them with jelly that old lady Eldon had put up. He poured some water out into cups for us and we sat down at the table and et all of it real fast.

"Where does your ma live, Robert?" Dewey asked, pulling out a chair and sitting down at the table with us.

"Mill Springs," I answered through my food. I couldn't stop to swaller it. I just kept chewing.

"Where's that?"

"North. We got to go to Marketville and change trains there . . ."

"You riding a *train?* Where'd you get the money?" Dewey asked, looking wide-eyed with surprise.

"We ain't got money," Abiah said and took a swaller of her water.

"We're riding the rails in boxcars," I told him with a grin.

"Hot dog!" Dewey cried. "Boy-howdy, riding the rails, now that's the life! How long you reckon it'll take to get to Mill Springs?"

I finished the last bite of my bread and jelly and said, "I'm planning on being at my ma's place on Christmas day."

"That's only ten days from now," Dewey said.

"Robert's going to get his ma a beautiful Christmas tree if she ain't got one already. Ain't you, Robert?" Abiah said and I nodded my head.

After we got our bellies full, Dewey wrapped some more bread and jelly in a sack for us to take with us and filled a Mason jar with water from the pump at the sink. He set the Mason jar into a sack and handed it to me.

By that time Mutt Dog (which is what we commenced to call him for his official name) had heard us and started howling and scratching at the kitchen door. Abiah went to the winder and tapped on it. "Hush up!" she called out and the dog quieted down.

"You reckon we ought to let him in?" Dewey asked.

"Naw. If old man Eldon is deef, just let the durned thing carry on," I told him.

"I sure am proud to see you, Robert," Dewey said with a grand big smile that went from ear to ear just about, and he reached out and punched my arm.

"How long you going to stay here, Dewey? You're big enough to run off now."

"I got the consumption, Robert. That's why the old lady don't bother on taking me out with the others."

I stared at Dewey. The cough, the pale, hollow cheeks and dark circles under his eyes . . . consumption! I felt something drain out of me, like as if it was my whole soul just falling away. Abiah moved close to me and in a small, dark voice said, "I feel bad for you, Dewey."

Dewey smiled big. "Hell, I'm having the best time I ever had in my whole life! Just screamin' in old man Eldon's ears is enough for me."

My heart squeezed up so tight I could hardly breathe. Screaming in the old man's ears! Sure didn't take much to make some people happy. But I reckoned Dewey was going to get his revenge on the old man before he passed on.

Dewey coughed and I heard it for the first time for what it really was. I'd heard the deep, gasping rattle before, from old folks who was dying. I never knowed no one so young as Dewey who had the consumption.

The grandfather clock struck the half hour. I looked at Abiah. "We'd better go," I told her and I glanced back at Dewey. His face was all pinched up from his cough.

Me and Abiah walked out of the house and into the yard with old Mutt Dog beating a path all around us, barking and carrying on. It was dark then and our new coats felt warm and snug against the wind. I give Abiah another look. She looked like a princess, all aglow in that red coat.

"I hope you have a good Christmas, Dewey," I told him, looking back at him standing in the doorway of the kitchen.

"Aw, don't worry about me! I'll have a fine Christmas," he said with a smile and a wave. "I hope the same for you-all and I hope you like your ma, B–Robert."

"Thank you for the coats," Abiah said gratefully and I seen how she snuggled more into it. It sure did make me feel good to see Abiah in that good red coat.

"Don't mention it. I sure do hope you get to your ma's by Christmas day, Robert," he called after us.

"We will!" I hollered over my shoulder. Then I hitched the sack of bread and the Mason jar of water up tight against my chest and grabbed Abiah's hand.

We run across the meadow to the stone wall, climbed over it, and hurried back in the direction of the train depot with Mutt Dog running ahead of us, then behind, and finally at our side. I was beginning to get used to him. Looked like he might turn out to be a good old mutt after all.

I pulled on Abiah's hand a little harder to make her run faster. We had to get to the depot before six o'clock to hitch the freight out of town.

Thing was, when we got to the depot and run down to the freight yard, they weren't but two boxcars on the tracks with no engine attached. It seemed awful peculiar and quiet to the way it was when we first pulled into town. Abiah and me exchanged a frown. Then I seen the shadder of someone inside the doorway of one of the boxcars. "There's someone," I said and we went up to the boxcar.

"Will the freight train going north be along soon?" I asked the man and he come out of the shadders and I could see he was all wore-out looking and his face was filled with heavy wrinkles. His clothes was all wrinkled too, like he'd been traveling a lot.

"Pulled out of here not fifteen minutes ago," he answered and his voice was as worn-out sounding as he looked.

"Are you *sure?*" Abiah asked.

"Well, sure I'm sure. Ought to know. I got off it. Rode it all the way from Upton Corners."

Me and Abiah sighed and looked at each other at the same time. Seemed like I could of cried if I hadn't had Abiah's hand to hang on to.

"Heard tell there's another faster freight later on tonight. A feller would be lucky to get on that one, though. It carries perishables and don't hardly stop for nothing."

"Thank you, sir," I told the man and we walked away real quick, before he could start asking *us* questions about why we wanted to know and what we was up to and such as that.

"Well, that's that," Abiah said.

"No, it ain't!" I said sharply. "I just got to think about what to do next, is all."

As we started to cross over the tracks, Mutt Dog jumped up my leg. I had to push him down, and when I did, the sack I was carrying broke and the Mason jar of water went crashing against the steel track. Mutt Dog rushed to it and started licking at the water.

"Come on," I said to Abiah. "Might as well try to warm up in the train depot while I think on this." I dropped the sack and shoved the bread Dewey had give us down in my coat pocket.

Chapter Eleven

When we went into the depot, Mutt Dog laid down outside the door and took the time to scratch at his fleas. The depot was warm and they weren't no one milling around. Except for the ticket agent behind the cage, me and Abiah was the only ones in there. While I was bent over with my chin poked down in my hands, thinking on what to do next, Abiah got up and went to look at the little Christmas tree that we'd seen from the winder when we first come into town. When the ticket agent seen her touching the ornaments, he asked her not to do it. "Why can't she? She ain't never had no Christmas tree to touch!" I wanted to snarl out at him, but I didn't. I just sat there and tried to enjoy the look on Abiah's face as she looked at everything.

Pretty soon the ticket agent barked, "I asked you not to touch them ornaments. They're old and might break." Then he commenced to study Abiah real close and to stare at me suspiciously. Finally he said, "Say, what are you kids hanging around here for? Where are your parents?"

Abiah turned around from the tree and answered, "We ain't got none. I mean, Robert's got a mother and we're going to see her."

The ticket agent rubbed his chin and squinted his eyes. "I heard the police was looking for two kids about your age. They stole some money from the mistletoe man and . . . "

Soon as he said that I jumped up, grabbed Abiah's hand, and out the door we went, lickety-split, running faster than a tumbleweed can be pushed by the wind. Mutt Dog was at our heels, follering us as we beat it alongside the railroad tracks and blasted right out of that town. After a while we was overcome by the darkness and quietness. They wasn't a light nowhere. Abiah commenced to fuss and grumble.

"I want to go back. It's too dark and spooky out here. It's like a wilderness," she said.

"You're as bad as old Grady, always trying to scare me, talking about ghosts and such. They ain't nothing out here but these old railroad tracks."

"Maybe if we went back we could wait for the freight in a boxcar and . . . "

"And have the police come looking for us. Didn't you *hear* that old ticket agent? He said the police was looking for two kids. If you ain't forgot about it, them two kids is *us!* You want to go back and get picked up and have the police send us back to Phineas and Earlene? Or maybe they'd send us to someplace that's even worse."

"No! Good or bad, I ain't never going to live in no foster home again! I done made up my mind to that."

"Then I reckon you'll have to go along with me and Mutt Dog."

"Well . . . well, I reckon I will," Abiah said with a resigned sigh.

We follered the tracks for a couple of miles, it seemed like. Then we crossed over a wide field that was all muddy from the winter wet and cold, and tramped through it looking for shelter. But they weren't none. It was just all open field. Finally we sat down on some tree stumps and rested, but it was too cold to sit for very long so we got up and started walking back to the railroad tracks. I reckon we walked ten miles or more, follering them tracks in the blackness and cold. Leastways it seemed that many.

"What are we going to do, Robert?" Abiah kept asking and I kept saying we was going to hitch on to that early morning freight when it come along. I didn't know *how* we was going to do it, but I had to tell Abiah we would, just to keep *my own* hopes up. The next day would make it nine days till Christmas. We *had* to get on that freight!

We didn't pay much attention to Mutt Dog until we come upon some bushes that growed close to the tracks and he started to sniff and poke around at them. His tail was all stuck up in the air and he kept going back and forth with his nose skittering over the ground. Pretty soon he started in to barking. Me and Abiah stopped and listened. We could hear voices coming up from behind the bushes and, when I moved closer to them I could see the flicker of firelight.

"Whoever's out there, come on down here!" a coarse-sounding man's voice called out. "If you're the laws, no need to worry. We ain't up to nothing."

"Don't go!" Abiah pleaded, pulling at my arm.

"We got Mutt Dog. We'll be okay," I told her, trying to sound brave.

The three of us plowed through the bushes and walked down an embankment until we could see the glow of the fire real good. Setting around it was three rough-looking men. We knowed right away they was hobos, just like the ones we seen riding the rails and sneaking in the boxcars at the Alberta Falls switching yard. One of them was wearing a dark, rumpled-looking suit jacket over overalls and a town gent's hat with a brim on it. We could see the hat was soiled and wilted looking. He wore a red kerchief around his neck, too. He had deepset dark eyes and heavy eyebrows and hair that straggled down below that hat. Next to him, setting on a bedroll, was a younger-looking man wearing khaki pants and a plaid jacket and a bill cap. He had heavy whiskers all over his face. The hobo next to him had on overalls and a long overcoat that was missing all the buttons. He had whiskers, too, and a short beard, and was chewing on something a mile a minute. I took it all in, wondering if these men was on the run from the laws like the hobo that took our corn bread on the freight from Temple was.

Old Mutt Dog stood in front of me and Abiah, growling and baring his teeth like if anyone tried something, he'd tear them into noodle strips.

"Well, looky yonder, would you? It ain't the laws, after all. It's two kids and a little old mean-looking dog!" the man with the red kerchief around his neck said and chuckled. The other two men chuckled along with him.

"He's as mean as he looks, too!" I said. "A dog don't have to be big to be mean."

Abiah tugged at my coat sleeve. I could tell she wanted me to be quiet, but I figured if I acted as much like a toughie as Mutt Dog was, we'd be a lot better off.

"The boy's right," the man in the overcoat said. "Come on down here and set by the fire."

I swallered hard, took in a deep breath and started walking toward the three hobos. Abiah stumbled along beside me, pulling back on me as much as she could. Mutt Dog walked right next to me with that mean growl still in his throat. When we reached the campfire, we could feel the warmth flutter over us. It felt so good, Abiah couldn't hold back from it. She moved a little closer and stuck out her hands. Mutt Dog went up beside her, like he was protecting her, and stood with his tail and ears standing straight up. I stood real close to them and stuck my hands out toward the fire too.

"Where you kids headed, anyway?" the man chewing so hard asked and he spit right into the fire. The fire sputtered for a second and a little whirl of smoke went rising into the air.

"Up the country," I answered stiffly, not wanting to get too friendly with them fellers.

"How fur up the country?" the man in the khaki pants asked.

"As far as Mill Springs," I answered.

"Purty fur to go in winter. Over three hundred miles or thereabouts."

Three hundred! The man with the red kerchief leaned over and pulled a can of beans out of a dirty satchel that sat on the ground next to him. It had already been opened. He stuck his fingers down in it and brought some beans up to his mouth. Looked like he swallered them down in one gulp!

"Don't matter if it's spring ner winter, and if it is three hundred miles, that's where we're going," I told them.

"How you expect to get there? Walk?" the man in the overcoat asked and they all laughed like as if it was some big joke.

"Going to ride the rails, that's how," I told them real sharp. "Just like we rode into Alberta Falls."

The men turned and looked at each other. Reckon they didn't feel like laughing then. Reckon they could tell we was experienced riders. I stuck my chest out and lifted my chin up high.

"Well, we got a flat wheeler coming on close to morning," the man in the overcoat said and he spit on the ground that time.

"What's a flat wheeler?" Abiah spoke up for the first time.

"A highballer," the bean eater saump 'It'll beat hell out of the tracks at up to sixty miles per hour. Got to be ready to jump it and ride rough."

"Reckon you can do it?" the spitter asked.

"We can ride rough as anybody," I answered with my chest and chin still stuck out.

"That dog there, you aimin' to take him with you?" khaki pants wanted to know.

"Yep," I answered.

"He'll be a mess of trouble," bean eater said, dripping bean juice from his fingers.

"He's already been," I had to admit.

"You kids hungry? Got another can of beans here," bean eater offered, but I told him we had our own food and felt in my pocket for the jelly and bread. The jelly got all sticky on my fingers, but I didn't care.

The other two hobos took food out of their belongings and commenced to eat, too.

Me and Abiah and Mutt Dog moved a little way off to ourselves and sat down in the dirt. The fire crackled and spit a little and burned brightly as we watched the three hobos go at their food. They was all finished in no time and pitched their cans into the bushes. They wiped their mouths on their coat sleeves and leaned back to relax.

I pulled out the sticky bread and give Abiah a slab and pinched off a little of mine for Mutt Dog. We et as fast as the hobos and in a second the bread was gone and Mutt Dog was whining for more. Abiah pulled him up to her and made him lay down. Then she curled up and used his back for a piller.

"Remember Miz Lottie Shamlin, Robert?" Abiah asked with her breath blowing out a little smoky drift into the cold air.

"Uh-huh," I answered, half drowsy.

"She were the beautifulest lady I ever seen. Someday I'm going to have long hair just like hers and wear fine clothes and smell just like she always smelled," she said in a dreamy, wistful way.

"You smell okay," I said and yawned. I didn't reckon it hurt to lie a little under the circumstances.

"Someday I'm going to talk just like her too and say 'yoo-hoo' and move around like a little breeze. I'll take baskets of food to poor folks and visit orphan homes and pray for the sick, just like she done."

I looked at Abiah. Her short hair was all splattered out over her head in them wild, wind-blown tangles. She looked a pure sight. I couldn't hardly imagine her looking as ladylike as Miz Shamlin.

"Which do you want the most, Abiah, to set in a red velvet winder seat and watch your ma and pa come in the yard and have a little sister not look like a doll no more or to be a fine lady like Miz Shamlin?" I asked, but she had closed her eyes and didn't answer.

"Well," I said under my breath as I watched her face resting against Mutt Dog's back, "if it be possible, I wish you both."

Chapter Twelve

I looked at the fire. It was burning low. Mutt Dog sniffed the damp dirt and scratched his nose with his paws. Abiah moved a little against his back as he moved. I reached out and patted his head and he looked up at me like he was pleased. It sure would be good to get to Mill Springs, I thought. But three hundred miles! Sure seemed like a long way to have to go. And what if we got to Marketville and they wasn't no freights out of there for days? I couldn't keep from worrying about that. But when I thought about my ma, I didn't worry so much. Seemed like thoughts of her soothed me. I had to smile, too. She was going to faint right out of this world when she seen me and found out who I was! She was going to laugh and cry and carry on and call in her neighbors and tell them about me! She was going to grab me and *never* let me go! I tried to think on what my first words to her was going to be, but all at once one of the hobos commenced to holler.

"It's comin'! It's comin'!" It was khaki pants, jumping up off his bedroll and tucking it under his arm. I sat up straight and watched him.

"How you know it's comin'?" bean eater asked, looking annoyed.

"I can feel it rumblin' in my feet! It comes right up through the ground into the soles of my feet, I tell you!"

"Aw, you're crazy as a bedbug!" spitter snorted, but he turned to look out toward the railroad tracks just the same.

"Crazy as a bat!" bean eater said.

It didn't matter what them other two hobos said. Khaki pants had already stomped off through the bushes. It was all quiet then. I looked at Abiah. She was still sleeping. But Mutt Dog had raised his head and commenced to whine a little.

Next thing I knowed, spitter was jumping up and shouting, "Hey, did you hear that?"

"What?" bean eater asked, but then he heard something too and jumped up. "It's the flat wheeler!" he cried and commenced to throw dirt on the fire and grab up his satchel. "Wasn't so crazy after all." He looked over at me and Abiah. "Better get a move on! She'll be slowing down when she reaches the turn just a little ways off. Soon as she reaches here she'll start to pick up speed. We got to run for it and be ready before she lays on the steam!"

I jumped up and shook Abiah. "We got to go! The train is coming!"

She leaped up before she was even wide-awake and we shot off through the bushes behind the hobos with Mutt Dog barking and running like a streak.

Sure enough, the flat wheeler was coming! We could hear it clattering along the tracks. Soon as we reached the clearing where we could see the tracks good, we seen the light from the engine pierce the darkness. She sped toward us like a mammoth creature, hugging the tracks and roaring out of the deep of night. When she got closer she slowed, just like the hobo said she would, and her brakes ground into the track with a shrill, inhuman-sounding cry. The three hobos moved around excitedly, bouncing up and down, walking back and forth, like their feet couldn't stay still. I felt my mouth go dry and my heart start to pound. I looked at Abiah and gripped her hand. Her mouth was hanging open as she watched the great train get closer. Mutt Dog was still, with his ears standing up. All at once she was upon us, slowing down . . . slowing . . . slowing more . . . more . . . and more!

"Now!" khaki pants cried and we all leaped toward the train where one of the boxcars doors was wide open and where hands and arms plunged out through the inner darkness to grab us and lift us up. One . . . two . . . three . . . all the hobos was pulled up and disappeared into the blackness of the boxcar. A second more and one . . . two . . . three . . . Abiah was yanked up into the boxcar. I grabbed Mutt Dog, hardly stopping my run, and held him with one arm while I stretched out my other one. Just a moment more and suddenly . . . suddenly the great train clanked and bellered and picked up speed.

"Grab a-holt!" "Grab my arm!" "Drop the dog!" "Hurry!" The yelling out at me from the boxcar was as loud as the train hammering on the tracks. But it weren't just the three hobos and their hands reaching out for me. Other hands and other voices come clamoring out, yelling frantically at me, and in it all was Abiah's voice screaming my name, "Robert! . . . Robert!" But suddenly her voice sounded further and further away and soon was gone and lost in the clashing of the steel wheels as they careened down the tracks.

I run and run, dropping Mutt Dog and clutching for the steel ladder, trying to grip on to anything and leap into the next boxcar or the next, but then I couldn't run no more. My breath was all gone, and the train was gone, and with it Abiah.

I stumbled to a stop and held my hands against my chest. My heart was pounding so hard it felt like it would beat its way right out of me! At my feet, Mutt Dog barked and nipped at my pant legs.

"No!" I hollered out to the wilderness that surrounded me. "ABIAH! ABI . . . AHHHHHHHHHH!"

After a little the night was silent. Even more silent than it had been before the train came crashing down the track. I looked around, swiping and trying to scratch away the tears that squawled out of my eyes. They weren't nothing but blackness. The sky met the earth in blackness and they weren't no difference in either one.

When I got my breath back I leaned down and picked up Mutt Dog. He shoved his head against my neck and whined. He knowed Abiah was gone.

"I knowed she couldn't jump. Not without me. I know she never would of stayed on that train if she could of jumped off. She was too afraid," I told Mutt Dog. And I thought sorrowfully, *Abiah . . . Abiah . . . what is going to happen to you?*

Chapter Thirteen

I started lumbering along the railroad tracks like some worn-out old hobo that had rode the rails too long. Seemed like all my strength and energy had run right out of me. But I knowed I was going north in the direction of Mill Springs and if I stayed close to the tracks, they'd get me out of all that wilderness into the next town. I carried Mutt Dog as far as I could, talking to him about Abiah. Now that she was gone, he was all I had. I never had no heavier feeling of being alone in my life ner of fretting over another person as I did after that flat wheeler charged away, carrying Abiah with it. I could imagine her packed into that boxcar with a hundred mean-looking hobos. I could see her eyes all big and frightened out of her wits, her hair in her face and that red coat wrapped around her, as I walked in the cold darkness.

"It's okay, Abiah . . . you'll be okay. Ain't no one going to bother you. Why, them old hobos, they just ridin' the rails, trying to get from one place to the other. They wouldn't bother you for nothing in this world." I talked out loud to that frightened face in front of me and Mutt Dog whimpered. "Looky here, me and you, we're going to meet up again and it won't be long, neither. I'll be looking for you and I'll find you. Don't you worry none about that. You hear me, Abiah?" I went on and all of a sudden I yelled out into the face surrounded by that darkness, "YOU HEAR ME, ABIAH RINGER?" and Mutt Dog wiggled out of my arms and went plunging to the ground.

"I sure do wish Reverend Shamlin was here to say some prayers for Abiah. Reverend Shamlin was real good with them prayers even if they didn't fit sometimes," I said, lowering my voice and looking down at Mutt Dog. My throat was so sore from bellering out for Abiah that I sounded like someone else talking. Mutt Dog give out a little bark. He knowed what I was talking about, all right. "We got to go on to my ma's, you know that, don't you, Mutt? We got to do that, but we'll stop in every town we come to and look for Abiah. She ain't going to stay on that train forever."

And that's what we done. First thing, when we walked into Morgantown, after walking most of the night and sleeping under someone's porch on a farm and skedaddling out and away soon as we heard the first rooster crow in the morning. By the time we come into town, I felt like my nose and ears was about froze off. I'd lost my old dog-eared cap and my hair must of looked like a whirlwind had run through it, judging from the way folks stared at me as they passed us on the street. We passed a cafe that had the smell of bacon and eggs rolling out of it and made my mouth tremble for the taste of food.

They was some old men setting in chairs leaned back against one of the buildings we passed, whittling on sticks and smoking cigars. One of them looked up and said, "That's a fine-looking dog you got there, young feller. What's his breed?"

"Mutt," I said and all them old men chuckled and looked at each other. "That's his name, too," I said and they chuckled again.

"How come he's so skinny?" one of them asked.

"'Cause he ain't et in a coon's age," I told him.

"How about you? You et recently?" another old man asked.

"No, sir, I ain't," I answered honestly.

"Well, here, you go and take this over to Jill's Cafe there next to the hardware store and buy you some bacon and eggs and tell Jill Henry Cromley said to give your dog a bone with some meat on it to gnaw on," that Henry Cromley said as he fished a bill out of his pocket and handed it to me.

"Thank you, sir," I told him and me and Mutt Dog hustled back to that cafe we first passed. But before we got there I heard one of them men say, "Wonder where that boy comes from? Don't seem right for a kid like that to come wandering into town hungry and looking so raggedy."

"Lots of young'uns out wandering around hungry nowadays. It's the times."

"You reckon he could be a runaway?"

When I heard that, I reckoned me and old Mutt had better grab us a quick sandwich at Jill's Cafe and get going. They wouldn't be time to eat bacon and eggs, not if the laws come looking for me. Old Phineas could of turned me and Abiah in or maybe old lady Eldon come home and found out about the coats from Dewey. I doubted Dewey would tell, but I wasn't going to hang around that town for long to find out.

I made Mutt Dog wait outside while I went inside Jill's Cafe and ordered a big beef sandwich. It come right up, real fast, and I got a drink of water from Jill, too. It sure felt good to be warm and to smell all them good food smells. I got back some change and shoved it down in my pocket, then I hurried outside and tore off a piece of the beef in the sandwich and give it to Mutt Dog. He wolfed it down in one gulp. I et mine just about that fast.

Before we headed back to the railroad tracks, I took a quick look around town, then hustled down to the train depot after a feller told me where it was. I figured if Abiah got off in Morgantown, she might be at the depot, thinking I'd show up there. I looked all over and didn't see no sign of her. Finally I asked everyone I seen that looked like they worked around the depot, but they all said they hadn't seen no young girl wearing a red coat that looked like I described Abiah. "Well," I told Mutt Dog, "may as well head on out." And we did.

We follered the railroad tracks past the town and out to where we could see farms and houses and fields plowed under for the winter and we walked past all that out where they wasn't nothing no more but barren land and the wind whipping at us more cold and raw and biting than it had been the night before. I picked up Mutt Dog and tried to stuff him under my coat to keep him warm, but he was too big and I couldn't walk against the wind carrying him. Finally I had to put him down and neither one of us could move but a little at a time without the wind trying to push us back. The wind whistled and yelled all around us and Mutt Dog commenced to whine and stopped walking. "Come on!" I shouted at him and the wind filled up my mouth and I could hardly stand up. "Come on, I said!" But he just sat there and stared at me with them big eyes. "Dang it, what's wrong with you?" I managed to shout again. Finally he got up and started trotting along behind me.

After pushing and shoving against the wind for a long, long time, we come to an old, tumbledown-looking wood bridge with a roof that was half rotted away. It had tree branches sticking down through it and they was bushes and ivy growing all around it. Well, I thought, it didn't offer much shelter from the cold and wind, but they might be some. I lumbered toward it and Mutt Dog follered me with his hair blowing like waves across his back. When we got to it, I slumped down on the bridge and felt a little of the wind leave me. Mutt Dog jumped into my lap and nuzzled real close. I scratched his head and rubbed his back and after a little he stopped shaking.

"You're a good old feller," I told him. It felt good just to be stopping, not to be running.

The wind was blowing so hard by then, the old bridge seemed to creak and rock each time it hit it. When I had my breath, I looked down past the rotting railings and seen that the pond below was all frozen over.

"Well, at least we ain't down there," I said to Mutt Dog, and all at once, for a reason I don't know, Mutt Dog jumped out of my arms and leaped up to the railing. I reached out for him, shouting for him to come back, but he didn't have no chance to obey me. All of a sudden the rotted wood railing crumbled like sawdust against his weight and fell away. Mutt Dog went falling with it, tumbling down into the icy pond below.

"Mutt Dog!" I shouted as I jumped up. But as I did, my weight caused a piece of the bridge beneath my feet to crack away and fall into the pond. I let out a wild yelp, sprang away from the spot, and looked down, searching for Mutt Dog and for a way to get down to the pond.

But they weren't no way. It was surrounded by a steep, muddy embankment, so slick, I knowed if I tried to get down it I'd go tumbling right into the pond same as old Mutt Dog done.

I stood there staring down into the frozen ice of the pond. They weren't no movement of no kind. Only a little hole where Mutt Dog had fell through. I stayed there for as long as I could stand it, hoping and praying old Mutt Dog would suddenly come leaping and yapping out of the hole, begging the Lord for one of them miracles Reverend Shamlin and all them other preachers that come to the foster homes used to talk about. But none come. Looked like I was never going to see that old dog again. He was gone just like Abiah was gone.

But wait! I told myself, maybe he could make it out of the pond down somewheres further. No, I guess there weren't no use to hope.

"Why'd you have to go and fall, you stupid old mutt? You crazy old dog! You didn't have no better sense than to fall in!" I bellered out over the wind and coldness and icy stillness of the pond. Wasn't no point in it, though. All the bellering in the world wouldn't bring no one back. I started walking gingerly off the bridge and, soon as my feet touched the ground, I looked up and seen a sign nailed to the trunk of a tree: DANGER—UNSAFE.

Mutt Dog couldn't read. But I could. If I'd only seen the sign! If I'd only been looking!

Chapter Fourteen

Walking alone is hard when you ain't got no old mutt dog pal to foller along with you, to bark and whine and nip at your pants every now and then. If I could of knowed Mutt Dog died soon as his head hit the ice, I sure would of felt better. I hoped he hadn't lived for one second even, in that burning cold water under the ice. I wished again that Reverend Shamlin was there to say some prayers. Even one about forbearing would of been okay. I reckon Mutt Dog wouldn't of minded none about that. He probably would of liked Reverend Shamlin and nipped at his pants a little. I walked on, pushing against the wind and feeling a dark, cold loneliness for Abiah and Mutt Dog.

After a little I heard the whistle of a train piercing the wind. The wind was whistling too, so it was hard to figure which direction the train was coming from. I stopped and listened real hard. Finally I could tell it was coming from behind me, in the direction I was headed. I started running like a streak, so fast it felt like the wind was jerking my hair right off the top of my head. I knowed I weren't too far from the tracks and when I found them, I waited, trying to catch my breath.

Soon the train, a great giant, came puffing down the tracks toward me. When it got close, I seen it was a passenger train. I watched and hoped they would be a boxcar or two on it and I prayed I'd be able to jump up on it when it passed. I spit into both my hands and rubbed them together. Sure enough, here come some boxcars at the end of the train. The train slowed a little and I reckoned they was a crossing down the way because I could hear a clanging noise. I missed the first boxcars, but I managed to leap up and grab ahold of the iron ladder on the side, grip it, and hoist myself up. I hung on to the ladder with all my might while I skinnied the little way across the boxcar and made a flying leap through the wide-open door.

I hit the floor inside with a painful *thump*, and when I did, musty-smelling cinders come soaring up all around me and landed in my face and mouth and all over me. The boxcar smelled like a hundred unwashed hobos had been living in it for a month with the door closed! But it appeared like I was the only one in it then. I rubbed the cinders out of my eyes and crawled over to the door and looked out. The train was moving so fast that everything looked like it was dancing past my eyes. I laid there with the wind whipping at me, watching the sky. It was filled with black clouds traveling toward each other. The rain was going to come, and come hard. Only good thing about that was, the rain would break the wind. But I couldn't let no rain ner wind slow me down. I'd have to get off at the first town the train come to and look for Abiah, just praying she would be there.

The train plowed on through the rest of the day and night and into the next day. I seen dawn come up all dim and wet, seen dancing trees and farmhouses and lakes and every now and then someone trudging along a highway with a pack on his back. The rain blowed through the boxcar door and all over me, making the cinders stick to my skin and clothes. I got up and moved far back into the car, trying to keep dry. It didn't do much good. Seems like the rain didn't have nowhere to go but inside the boxcar. I couldn't keep warm ner dry ner get comfortable in any way. I was hungry and sick with worry over Abiah. I closed my eyes and her face come before me again. Her eyes was all wide with fear. Then I seen old Mutt Dog's face. I rubbed and rubbed at my eyes, trying to take away the tormented look on it, trying to forget seeing him crash through the side of the bridge and trying to forget the sound of Abiah's voice screaming out my name as the train fled away from me.

The next day, when we pulled into a place called Clovis Hill, I was so hungry, my stomach was playing with my backbone. It had commenced to snow. I reckoned, since leaving the Hicksons, I'd met up with just about every temperature and type of weather they was. All I could do was take the snow in my stride and keep going. Seemed like I'd walked and rid them freights a million miles already. I had to get to Mill Springs! But I knew I had to get something to eat before I dropped over.

When I jumped out of the boxcar and scrambled around, making my way into town, I knowed I looked even worse than any old hobo ever could. I seen myself in the shop winders on the main street, walking along, looking like a fool with the snow falling, and me all packed down with cinders. The coat Dewey give me stuck to me like a glob of glue and smelled about as bad. My pants was tore at the knees and my brogans had come to the end of the line as far as anyone ever wearing them again. I was a sight, all right, but I couldn't let the way I looked stop me.

The street looked like a picture in a book with the winders of the shops all decorated with shining lights and wreaths on the doors and people passing up and down dressed real warm, wearing nice clothes and carrying packages. I stopped at a place that said it was Dokstadders Clock Repair Shop and peered through the winder. An old feller wearing glasses was behind a counter tinkering with what looked like a tore-apart clock. On the wall behind the counter a lot of different-shaped clocks hung. Didn't look like they was no customers in there and the old man looked all right to me, so I decided to open the door and go inside and ask about Abiah. Maybe I could warm up a little too. Soon as I walked through the door, the old feller looked up and studied me over the top of them glasses.

"Excuse me, sir, but I was wondering if you seen a girl around town here wearing a red coat," I said as I walked up to the counter. I was trying to shake the snow out of my hair at the same time.

The old gent laid what was in his hand down and said, "No, I can't say as I remember seeing a girl in a red coat."

"She'd have short stringy hair, real fine and straight as a string," I told him.

He nodded like he was thinking about it. Then he frowned. "No, I don't recall such a girl. She live in Clovis Hill?"

"No, sir, she'd be just passing through, stopping off here awhile."

"Not many folks stops off in Clovis Hill. Most folks that come and go around here lives right here."

"Well . . . if you see this certain girl, would you tell her Robert is looking for her?"

The old feller come around from behind the counter and pushed his glasses up on his nose. He had a mighty curious look on his face. I wondered if I was wrong about him.

"Where did you come from, Robert? You look awful wore out for a young boy."

I didn't want to tell him no details about where I come from so I just said, "I'm passing through town. Come from a town over yonder . . ." I jerked my arm out and pointed toward a side wall of the shop which was in a south direction. Then I started to back off toward the door. The old man moved closer.

"Wait a minute, Robert. I can see you're in bad need of a change of clothes. That jacket you're wearing is all soaked and it's bound to get soaked even more with the way it's snowing out there. My daughter has a dry goods store across the street." He nodded toward the front winder and I looked. Colored Christmas lights around the winder made the snow twinkle all reds and greens and blues. The snow was coming down heavier and made me shiver just to think about going out in it again.

"Let me take you over there to Ella's store and get you fitted for a heavy coat. You need some dry pants, too, and some shoes," the old man went on.

"Well, I'm obliged to you for the offer, sir, but . . ."

He eyed me closely. "I don't know if you're a runaway or just a homeless boy and it don't matter. Folks in Clovis Hill are noted for helping children out. I'll just pull on my overcoat . . ."

I stared at that old man with a sharp eye. Folks in Clovis Hill are noted for helping kids out . . . I had to think on that. It sounded mighty suspicious to me. Kids like me didn't get much help from no one less'on they was being paid by the county.

I didn't know what to say so I didn't say nothing. I stood there watching as he pulled on his coat and cap and wrapped a long knit scarf around his neck. When he was ready, he put a sign in the winder that said he would be back later and we walked out the door.

I'd lost track of time and needed to know the date. "What calendar day is it, sir?" I asked while he bent down to lock the shop door.

"Why, don't you *know,* son? It's December twentieth, the year of our Lord nineteen and thirty-two."

The twentieth of December! I only had five days to get to Mill Springs if I didn't count that day.

"Sir, do you happen to know of a town called Mill Springs?" I asked this as we crossed over the street. The wet snow was gushing up into the soles of my old, ragged brogans and falling into my eyes and mouth when I talked.

"Yes, I've heard of the place."

"Is it far from here?"

"It would likely take awhile to get there from here. We've a big mountain between. It would probably be faster by train than by car."

We walked up on the sidewalk and the old feller pulled the door of the dry goods store open for me. He motioned for me to go inside and he follered me.

"Ella! Ella, we've got a customer out here!" he called into the store. All around was tables loaded up with clothes and some was on hangers too. They was a shelf of shoes along the wall and another shelf with hats on it. They was even pictures on the walls. The smell of coffee mixed with the smell of the shoes and clothes.

After I'd run my eyes all around over everything, I seen a little thin lady come out from a door at the back of the store. She wore a dark dress and her hair was pulled back into a knot at the back of her head. She had a friendly smile on her face.

"Ella," the old man said, "this is Robert." And he touched my shoulder with his hand. It were only a touch, but it felt like a granpa hand might feel, and I warmed up to it.

"Hello, Robert," Ella said with her friendly smile and she walked up to me and put out her hand. I took it and give it one shake and she hung on to it and put her other hand over the top of it. "Robert, how *cold* you are," she said and she was leaning down, looking right into my eyes. Her hand was so warm it felt like a glowing fire, already warming me up.

"Robert could use a pair of mittens, Ella. And some shoes and pants and a jacket . . . " the old feller said and Ella went on with, "And a nice snug cap and scarf, too, Papa."

I had to gulp down a swaller! I never run into no one so kind and generous before, without they was only play-acting. All my life I'd reckoned I'd already run out of luck before I even got any!

Well, them two, Dokstadder, the old clock man, and Ella, his daughter, they fixed me up like some city feller, in fine warm clothes and even throwed in a pair of long johns and socks. By the time I was all dressed up, I didn't feel like myself no more. They was a mirror on a door and Ella told me to look in it and see how I liked myself. I felt kind of silly to do it with them two watching, but I was curious, so I did it. When I seen how I looked, I wondered who that boy in the mirror really was. Was he *me* or a new boy that stepped into me, took my mind and thoughts, and plunked them into his body? I sure was a sight!

Before I left the dry goods store, Ella had give me hot coffee and enough cookies to stuff me good and some to put in my pocket for later. Then the clock man, Mr. Dokstadder, he pushed two real one-dollar bills into my new jacket pocket.

By that time I was starting to feel guilty for all they give me. "I can sweep out the store for you and . . ." I started in to say, but the clock man touched my shoulder again. "Robert," he said, "take whatever kindness you receive in life and pass it on to someone else. From that, a long chain of kindness will grow and, who knows? Maybe one day it will cover the whole earth."

Well, he sure said some good words, all right, things to think on.

When I left them two, I felt like I was ready to lick the world. New clothes give to you free, and goodness thrown in, sure can make a difference in a poor feller's life. On top of that, Ella kissed me goodbye on both cheeks and then, after she'd twisted the new blue scarf around my neck and pulled the matching cap over my head, she give me a big popping kiss on my forehead.

As I started out the door, I heard Ella say with the sound of concern in her voice, "Where do they all come from, Papa, and where do they all go, these roving bands of children we clothe and feed and send on their way?"

I closed the door before I could hear the old feller's answer.

Chapter Fifteen

It looked like December twentieth was my lucky day. The snow had let up and when I walked down the street, looking at all the Christmas decorations in the stores and keeping a wide eye out for Abiah, I come upon a group of carolers standing on the sidewalk singing.

> *"Hark! the herald angels sing,*
> *Glory to the newborn King;*
> *Peace on earth, and mercy mild . . ."*

The sound of their voices trilled so warm and sweet that I had to stop and listen. They was six of them singing, all young, but older than me, and a man and a woman holding songbooks. When they finished one song they commenced right into another one:

> *"O come all ye faithful,*
> *joyful and triumphant,*
> *O come ye, O come ye to Bethlehem . . ."*

I couldn't keep from humming along with them. Next thing I knowed, my mouth was opened wide as theirs and I was singing out like a fury:

> *"Come and behold him,*
> *born the King of angels . . ."*

Just before we got to the end of the song, the man holding a songbook reached out and pulled me right into the carolers and, next thing, there I was, looking out at all the people that had formed to listen and I was singing like a songbird itself had flew into me and I couldn't keep still.

A little while later, after we'd all sung ourselves out, the man that had pulled me into the group said, "I don't know where you come from, but you sure are a blessing to us, young man. One of our best singers is home sick. No telling when he'll get well enough to sing again. How about you taking his place? Come and go with us to Clement's Pond. It's not far . . ."

"In what direction is it, sir?" I asked. "Is it on toward Mill Springs?"

"In that direction," he answered and everyone started clamoring for me to go there and sing with them. But then suddenly the man raised up his hands for everyone to be quiet. "No, wait!" he said. "We've got to ask this boy's parents."

"I ain't got no parents, sir," I told the man. But then I thought about my ma and how I was trying to get to her and I added, "Leastways not here. I'm on my own." Everyone got quiet then and stared at me. "I can go anywheres I want to."

"How long have you been on your own, son?" one of the women asked.

"Ever since I can remember," I replied.

I noticed their eyes run up and down my new clothes, like they was wondering how I got them. Then another caroler said, "You must of met up with Presley Dokstadder and Ella."

"Yes, ma'am," I answered and I told them all about how the old clock man and his daughter had decked me out and treated me so fine.

"You're not the first one, and you won't be the last, to be helped by them," the man said. Then he asked my name and I told him what it was and he said, "Well, how about it? Will you go with us and sing Christmas carols in Clement's Pond?"

I thought about it. Sure would be nice to get on down the road closer to Mill Springs without having to ride in one of them boxcars and I'd have some friendly company besides. Thing was, though, I hadn't yet give a good look around town for Abiah. I couldn't leave without doing that first. "I got a friend I been looking high and low for. I got to try and find her before I leave," I said and the young people, they started in telling me they'd help me. They knowed the town like the back of their hand, they said, seeing as how it were their home, and could look places I couldn't. The man and woman agreed to that, but started in asking lots of questions. I told them as little as I could without making them too suspicious. Finally we all spread out, looking for Abiah. It didn't do no good, though. No one found her.

"If she was here, we would of found her," one of the carolers told me when we met back on the street a little later. "Everyone knows when there's a stranger in town," he added.

"Climb into the trucks," the man caroler called out and I follered them to the two trucks that was parked along the street and climbed into one.

It had stopped snowing altogether now and the sky had come out dark with sparkling stars. It was still cold, but I was warm in my new clothes and them mittens sure did keep my hands snug.

Well, all this is how I got on down the road a little further toward Mill Springs. When we got there, the town looked a lot smaller than Clovis Hill and they weren't many stores, just a few, but they was all decorated for the season and looked warm and nice. I liked it right well there and they was lots of people on the street. Looked like they was waiting for us to arrive and knowed all the carolers by name.

They was one old lady there, standing with a boy holding a lot of packages for her. She give us all an invite out to her house when we was finished singing. She said she'd give us hot cocoa and cake.

"I'm Ester Tarver," she said to me. "And this here is my nephew, Lyon." Her nephew was real slim and looked like he might still be growing. He acted shy except for when another feller come up and started joking with him. His name was Justin, Miss Ester said. Fact is, I would of liked to know them folks better, but I had to look around for Abiah. While everyone was talking and deciding if they'd go or not out to Miss Ester's place, I slunk away and took off to look around. My heart was heavy with thoughts of Abiah and what could of happened to her. While I was singing and having a high old time, *where was she?* I wondered. I tried not even to think about the hobos.

When I started past a place with a sign that said VI'S MILLINERY SHOP, I seen two girls come out the door and start ahead of me down the street. It was dark and I couldn't see them too well except from the lights in the shop winders. But one had on a red coat! Abiah!

"Abiah! Abiah!" I hollered and I started running toward the girls with my heart pounding. They didn't turn around. "Abiah! It's me! Robert!" I hollered again. By then I was so close I could of touched the cap on the head of the girl in the red coat. It covered her whole head and I couldn't see her hair, but I *knowed* it was Abiah.

"Abiah!" I said again and both girls turned around and looked at me. It *weren't* Abiah! The girl didn't have Abiah's face and the red coat she had on weren't old looking. It looked brand-new and I seen that it had big black buttons down the front.

"What do you want?" the girl in the red coat asked and she didn't act a bit friendly.

"I . . . I t–thought you w–was Abiah," I muttered.

"Well, she ain't Abiah! Her name is Taffy!" the other girl said in a snippy way. I looked at her long white hair that spread out on the shoulder of her coat and I thought it was lots more pretty than her sharp tongue.

"Come on, Sylvie," the girl in the red coat said and they whipped around and hurried off down the street.

I didn't go back to where the carolers was. I walked up and down the street, looking every which way for Abiah. She was nowhere to be seen. Soon I got so sleepy, I had to stop and set down in the doorway of a feed store. Them carolers must of thought I disappeared! Before I knowed it, I was asleep and I didn't wake up until the next morning, the twenty-first of December.

When I woke up and stood up to stretch, I seen an old man standing out by the curb spitting tobaccer juice into the gutter. He turned and looked at me and said, "It's a wonder you didn't freeze to death! I seen you over in that doorway before the rooster even crowed this morning. What's a boy doing in these parts sleeping in a doorway?"

I went up to him and dodged a flurry of spit that rushed past me. "I've been looking for a friend, sir," I said real polite. "She's wearing a red coat and has dark hair and . . ."

"That be Taffy. She ain't much of a friend to no one, though. Her ma won't let her be."

"It ain't her," I told him and I explained to him about Abiah and how I had to find her and get on to Mill Springs. And I asked, "What's the next town to here?"

"Next big place be Tylersville. Mill Springs is a little ways from there," he said and spit another good wad. This time flecks of the tobaccer juice landed on my jacket.

"I reckon I'll go over to the train depot," I said, "and hitch a ride on a boxcar."

"Ain't no train coming through here for two days. You might get a ride into Tylersville with George Goad. He runs the grocery. Takes his truck over there to pick up supplies. It being Tuesday, I reckon he'd be getting ready to go right now."

"Where's his store?" I asked with excitement running all through me.

"Right behind you," he said, pointing. "Tell him Oscar Bebee sent you to him."

"Yes, sir, thank you, sir," I said and I rushed right through the doorway of that store like a storm was at my heels.

Well, that's how I got me a way to the big city of Tylersville. That

George Goad, he was a nice feller, even bought me some lunch and wished me luck in finding my ma and Abiah. When we parted he called out after me, "Come on back to Clement's Pond someday. It's a good place to live. We'll make room for you!"

I smiled and waved at him as the truck pulled off.

Looking for Abiah in a place like Tylersville was even worse than trying to find a needle in a haystack. She just weren't nowhere to be seen ner was she heard of by anyone I talked to. Along about evening I come upon a rowdy-looking place with bright lights and a jukebox spewing out loud music. They was all kinds of men and women staggering in and out of the door. Just as I was passing, a big feller with a mean-looking face come out and give me a hard look. "You got any money?" he snarled at me.

"No, sir," I told him and I stuck my hand in my pocket real quick to cover the two dollars the clock man had give to me.

"What you got in that pocket?" he demanded, coming toward me.

"I ain't got nothing!" I lied and I started backing away, but he reached out and grabbed my arm and pulled me to him.

"You better give me what's in that pocket or I'll punch your teeth right out of your head!"

"I . . . I ain't got n–nothing, I told you!" I was shaking so bad I felt like a bowl of wobbling jelly!

"Don't you lie to me!" he yelled in my face as he yanked my hand out of my pocket. I had the two dollar bills crumbled up in my palm. He pried it open and punched me in my mouth. When I started falling to the sidewalk, he yanked off my scarf and knit cap and took off in a fast run down the street.

I touched my mouth and a tooth fell into my hand. It was one of the front ones. I shoved it down in my pocket and got up. It was the second time I'd had money stole from me. I wished I'd never seen Tylersville! But, if I'd knowed better, I reckon I wouldn't of been hanging around on a honky-tonk street. I reckoned the vacant spot in my gums would always remind me of my ignorance.

It sure did hurt to have a tooth knocked out and get stole from at the same time. Well leastways they weren't much blood to contend with!

I asked someone passing on the sidewalk where the train depot was. They told me, but I couldn't make it there. I felt too bad about the money and my knocked-out tooth. I commenced to shiver. Without my warm knit scarf and cap, the wind whipping at my ears and neck felt like I was being spanked with an apricot switch. I sat down on the curb, wondering what to do. I don't know how much time passed while I sat there, but after a while some old men come along, sat down near me, and commenced swigging on a bottle. I reckoned they was drunks and I was in the wrong place again. It sure was a sorry life. I reckoned I wished I was dead and out of my misery. But I knowed I had to find Abiah, and I had to get to my ma's in Mill Springs. It was all that kept me going.

Chapter Sixteen

In three days I'd be thirteen years old and in four days it would be Christmas. I commenced to fret on that real bad. I was so sick and sore from the hole in my gums from the tooth being knocked out that I couldn't do nothing but lay around dozing in doorways at night and beg for food in the daytime. I was in a dazed state, I reckon.

They was some folks give me a nickel and one or two that give me a dime. But mostly folks just ignored me. You see, I found out they was lots of fellers just like me, looking for a handout on the streets. Some was men, but they was lots of kids too. They was all dressed ragged and looked half starved. I guess folks got plumb tired of being asked for a handout on every corner.

I'd give up on begging, deciding it weren't a very profitable occupation, when I looked up on my second day in Tylersville and seen a young feller coming toward me on the sidewalk with a big smile on his face. He had red hair and red freckles and big hungry-looking green eyes. He had on a blue stocking cap and an old gray coat that looked like all them ratty coats on the floor at the Eldons' place. His pants was baggy and rolled up several times at the ankle. I reckoned they was too long for him. I could see his toes sticking out the end of one of his scruffy old shoes. But with all that, he appeared like a feller that might of sung a song or even whistled a tune. When he reached where I stood, he stopped and asked, "Having any luck?"

I knowed he meant on the begging. "Nope. Folks is as tightfisted as a cork in a jug," I answered.

"Come on with me. There's a better corner than this to stand on. If you have to beg, you've got to beg in the right place."

I follered him down a couple of blocks where they was more sidewalk traffic and folks looked more prosperous. They carried packages and wore furry muffs and overcoats and nice hats. Manikins in the shop winders was dressed like only rich folks could dress and all around them was Christmas decorations. Even the shop doors had huge holly wreaths on them. We stopped at the corner and the feller said, "My name is Stephen Skeffington the second. What's yours?"

That sounded like a mighty fancy name for a raggedy-looking kid like he was. Fact of the matter was he talked kind of fancy too. He even stood like he might of been as smart sounding as that name he had, tall and straight, with his chin up. Looked like life hadn't whupped him yet.

I give him my name and he asked right off, "Don't you have a last name, Robert?"

I studied on that, seeing as how "Robert" was all I ever went by. "Well," I said and hesitated, "my name *could* be Whitlaw."

"What do you mean, could be?" Stephen asked, looking curious.

That's when I told him about being in the foster homes and all that. It were the first time I'd told anyone about it and then I told him about Abiah and Mutt Dog and how I was trying to get to Mill Springs to be my ma's Christmas present. But I felt so sore and beat out that I didn't know how I was going to make it and try and find Abiah too. It all come rushing out of me like an avalanche of snow driving down a mountainside.

When I finished my spiel, Stephen plunged right into telling me his story. He said he had run away from his fancy New York home after his brother had been beat up in a boys' school, the same school his parents wanted him to go to. He told me his brother got his brain damaged from the beating and he refused to go there where he would have to see them same boys and know they had got away with it. "It's a tradition in my family, Robert. My great-grandfather was one of the founders of the school. My father and his father went there. But I refused to and left."

"Don't you miss all that money and stuff?" I asked, looking up and down his raggedy clothes.

He looked like he was studying on that hard. Then he said, "I only miss my brother. But he doesn't even know I'm gone."

Him saying that made me think of the fellers at the Hicksons', Luther and Grady and Jimmy. I was surprised when he said, "I'll help you, Robert. I know this town pretty well. And I know some kids I can pass the word around to. I'm sure they'd be willing to help look for Abiah. We'll have to hurry. That freight going north pulls out just after dark. I've hung around the freight yard enough to know."

Stephen took off then and I reckoned it was all an act and I'd never see that used-to-be-rich kid again. But weren't no time and here he come, follered by three young raggedy toughs, all looking big-eyed and scrawny. They come up the sidewalk and Stephen said, "These are my pals. They're going to help look for your friend." He started in to telling me their names. They was Willie, a short boy with dark eyes and long dark lashes and shaggy-looking hair that tumbled into his eyes. Then they was Brad, the tallest of the bunch, with a cautious eye that wouldn't stop staring at me. And they was Mark, who had a runny nose and kept wiping his coat sleeve over it. They all had on knit caps and looked about as poor as any kids I ever seen. Even me. They was all street kids, living in vacant buildings or sleeping in doorways, begging for or stealing food or digging in garbage for it when they couldn't get it no other way.

I give them Abiah's description and told them what she was wearing and Brad spoke up and said, "All right, boys, let's fan out! If she's here, we'll find her."

"And we'll pass the word around too," Mark said after a good swipe under his nose.

"We'll meet back here on this corner at dusk," Willie said.

The three fellers took off in different directions and Stephen went with me. We give a walk around in all the shops and was run out of most of them by the proprietors, stopped people on the streets, give out what Abiah looked like and her name, but everyone shook their heads. We went into churches and knocked on doors of houses on every street, but no one had seen her or knowed a thing about a girl in a red coat. I commenced to think Abiah hadn't come north after all, that she must of stayed on that freight and got switched onto another line that took her in a different direction. Or maybe one of them hobos took her somewhere with him or . . . But I didn't want to think about such things. I only wanted to believe that I would find Abiah and she would be all right.

One of the ladies at a house where we stopped sawed all the fat off some bacon pieces for us and poked it between slabs of hot bread.

"Here," she said, handing the bread out the door to us. "This fat will stick to your bones and keep you warm. I got to save the lean meat for my own kids."

We thanked her and was happy to get anything to eat, no matter what it was. She give us one sody water between us and we shared it.

When it come about dusk, we headed back to town to meet up with the boys. I prayed they would have some good news for me. When we reached the corner where we was to meet, the three fellers was already there. I could tell from the glum expressions on their faces they didn't have no better luck than me and Stephen had.

"We asked and looked and went everywhere," Brad spoke up when we reached them. "Even places most folks don't even know about."

"But she ain't here, less'on someone's holding on to her," Mark said. But I didn't want to think about that!

"Best thing for you to do is head on out for Mill Springs if you want to be there by Christmas day, Robert," Stephen said. "We'll keep looking for Abiah."

"You thinking on going to Mill Springs?" Brad asked. I nodded my head. "That means you got to go over Riley's Ridge."

"What's Riley's Ridge?" I asked.

"You'll soon find out if you ride the rails out of here. All the freights out of Tylersville stop there for a whole night, right at the very top of the mountain. I ain't seen it, but I heard tell it's like you been stranded up at the top of the world and one little creak of that old train, and *flueey!* Down you go, right off that ridge, all the way to the bottom of the canyon."

"I heard tell," Mark said with a sniff and a swipe across his wet nose, "that they was a feller got so scared up there, he went crazy and jumped right out of a boxcar over the ridge. Men in the boxcar that was with him seen him fall and they said he never did quit falling."

"Fact of the matter is, he's *still* falling," Willie added, looking as straight-faced and serious as you please. "He ain't never reached the bottom of that canyon. That's how far down it is from Riley's Ridge."

I had to gulp at everything they told me. It didn't make no sense, but what they said sure could scare a feller bad. I looked from face to face. Even Stephen's face had a serious expression on it.

"A–a whole night on top of that ridge?" I asked and all the boys nodded.

"But when you go down off Riley's Ridge and pull into the valley, you'll see the most beautiful place you could ever imagine," Stephen said. "And that will be Mill Springs." Hearing that made me feel a lot better.

All the boys walked me down to the train depot and kept a watch while I snuck onto one of the boxcars that was attached to the biggest engine I'd ever seen. It was as black as tar and looked like some animal right out of the dark ages. It give me a chill just to look at it. They was lots of brakemen walking around, carrying their lanterns, looking watchful. "Take care, Robert. You've got a long way to go," Stephen said in a quick, low voice. I only had time to thank him for his help before the loud sound of "GET THEM BOYS!" came traveling over the freight yard. Then, "THINK THEY'RE GOING TO GET A FREE

RIDE!" Next was, "THEY'LL GET A FREE RIDE, ALL RIGHT! RIGHT OFF TO THE CITY JAIL, WHERE THEY KEEP LITTLE HOOLIGANS ON THE RUN!"

I heard the boys scatter, the heels of their shoes scraping over the gravel that lay between the train tracks. I shrunk back into the shadder of the boxcar as far as I could, hoping the trainmen hadn't seen me climb into it. Soon I seen three or four breakmen hurrying past the open boxcar door, scraping their shoes in the gravel. "THEY MUST OF RUN DOWN THAT WAY!" I heard one of them blast out and I commenced to tremble with fear that they would catch the boys.

In the next minute I felt the scrape and grind as the huge train wheels started to move. They was a little jerk this way and a little jerk that way, starting up slow, then a sudden loud clang and heavy jerk and all at once the cold wind was pouring through the open door. From out of my dark corner I could see us moving past cars that sat still on the nearby tracks. L & M . . . B & O . . . Kansas . . . Southern Pacific . . . I tried to read the names printed on the cars, but we swept past too fast and everything turned into a blur. Then they was all gone. We was going full speed then, snorting past the dilapidated patchwork excuses for houses where the poor country folks lived, past acres and acres of barren fields, dead and cold with winter. Dark birds whooped and screeched out of the spindly, leaf-stripped trees and flew about the gloomy dark sky.

Finally I left the doorway and sat down. Someone had laid some cardboard out on the floor. It felt warm compared to the cold boxcar floor. I leaned against the wall, feeling lonesome and all alone in the world. Even more alone than I felt when I went them first days to all them foster homes. I felt sorry for myself and wanted to cry. Then I started thinking about Stephen and the other boys in Tylersville who had give me some feeling of friendship and lots of help. And I thought of the old clock man and Ella in Clovis Hill and how they had give me the new clothes, and the carolers and how they had welcomed me into their group like as if I was as good as they was. I commenced to think with a deep warmness of all of them. Maybe the world weren't so bad. Maybe they really was some good folks in it who didn't expect nothing from you, or even the county, when they did something for you.

In two days it would be Christmas Eve and I'd turn thirteen. Then it would be Christmas and, if all went right, I expected to be in Mill Springs with my ma. She sure was going to be surprised to see her son! I shut my eyes and could see how she would look, even though I didn't know what she really looked like. What I done was, I sort of put Abiah's face there to be ma's face, only older, and I talked to her and told her all I was going to do for her to help her out. In case she needed help, that is. And I told her she wouldn't never have to work hard again, provided she was working hard. I even told her if she was rich, not to worry about it. I weren't out after nothing she had except her love. That would always be enough for me.

I must of dozed a little because the next thing I knowed, I felt my head knock against the wall of the boxcar. We was whipping out now, soaring with speed, traveling like hell's own fury along the tracks. Everything outside the boxcar door just blew past like the wind. I couldn't even make out a tree. That's how fast that train was going. After a while I decided to lay down on the cardboard. I discovered they was two pieces so I took one and covered myself up with it. It weren't warm, but it was better than nothing and it did keep the wind whirling through the door off me.

The rattle, chug, and jerk of the train rocked me back to sleep and all I seemed to know for a long, long time was dreams. Long dreams of dancing Christmas trees with glittering lights and a woman in a print dress turning around and smiling at me. Her face was round and pretty and I seen my eyes in hers. It was my ma in my dream. Once, when I woke, the train seemed to be going at a slow pace. Seemed like then we was in a switching yard and cars was being taken off the train and others put on. I heard voices and saw the swish of lanterns outside the boxcar door, but I just laid there, like as if I couldn't come out of my dream.

On and on the train went, mile after mile, chuffing and hooting, clacking and bellering across my dream. One minute I raised my head and seen the light of day and the next minute my head was down on the cardboard again with my dream running back into my head.

It was the slanted feeling, the feeling of my body laying on the cardboard and standing against it at the same time that finally woke me up good. My eyes snapped open and I sat up, looking toward the boxcar door. Night had come again. I'd lost a whole day in my dream. I reckon I hadn't knowed how tired I was.

The boxcar was at a slant all right, and it were being pulled upward, huffing and puffing on the tracks like the engine could hardly haul the train. I shook the cardboard off me and tried to stand, but I couldn't. I tried to crawl across the floor to the door, but I couldn't do that neither. Alls I could do was pray the train weren't getting ready for a crash.

Then it struck me! Riley's Ridge! The train must be heading up Riley's Ridge! I shuddered and pulled the cardboard back over me, thinking about the crazy man who had jumped out of the boxcar that Mark had told me about. "He's still falling . . . he ain't never reached the bottom of the canyon," Willie had said. "All the freights out of Tylersville stop there for a whole night . . . right at the very top of the mountain . . . one little creak of that old train, and *flueey!*"

I was determined not to think on such things, but I listened for every little creak of the train that might send us over the edge of the tracks. Sometimes during that cold, dark night, I thought I could hear the crazy man yelling out from far far down in the canyon. It made me tremble just to think about it. But somehow or other I went back to sleep and when I woke up I could feel the train moving under me and see the brightness of another day falling through the boxcar door. I scrambled up and rushed to the door and looked out. Towering snow-covered mountains rose into the clouds on the other side of a deep, deep canyon that seemed to dive right into forever. I looked down and jumped back quick! The train tracks lay right at the very edge of the cliff. The crazy man didn't *jump* out of the boxcar, I thought. He must of *fell!* And maybe he weren't crazy at all.

I went back and sat down on the cardboard and pulled the other piece up against me to shield me from the sharp coldness. The boxcar suddenly turned in a downward slant like an airplane going into a nosedive. The wheels crackled on the tracks and the boxcar rattled and shook like it was ready to explode into a million pieces and go flying over into the canyon. I hung on to the cardboard for dear life and went tumbling to the end of the boxcar, hitting my head and shoulder against the wall. We was on our way now, plunging down, down, and even further down, headed for Mill Springs.

"I wish you was with me, Abiah. I wish you and Mutt Dog was both with me," I yelled out in fear, but the boxcar was making such a racket I couldn't even hear my own voice.

Chapter Seventeen

A feller don't know how wore out he is less'on he keeps on falling asleep, which is what I done over and over. Last time I woke on the train, it was to something that sounded like a stampede of cattle. My eyes flew open and I stared wide-eyed at a whole troop of men and boys about my age leaping up into the boxcar. I jumped up, afraid they'd run right over me if I didn't get out of the way. I rubbed my eyes and stumbled to the boxcar door, asking no one in particular where we was.

"Mill Springs, squirt!" a man's gruff voice shot out at me.

"Mill Springs?" I asked like I was in a stupor. Then I was wide-awake. Mill Springs! "What day is it?" I asked and someone answered, "It's Christmas Eve, you bozo!"

"*Christmas Eve?*" I shouted and sprang out the door, landed on my knees in the dirt, got up, and shouted again, "Mill Springs! Mill Springs! It's Christmas Eve and I'm in Mill Springs!"

I could hear everyone in the boxcar trampling to the door, listening and watching me. "Crazy as a loon!" someone said and everyone laughed, but I didn't care. Alls I cared about was that I was in Mill

Springs and it were Christmas Eve. I'd got there the day *before* Christmas! It weren't until I was skipping and dancing away from the railroad tracks that I realized it was my birthday too. I was thirteen years old! I started running like a whirlwind to the small depot, marched up to the cage inside where a ticket agent with a round, friendly face leaned toward me on the little counter.

"Could you tell me, sir, where the Whitlaws is living?" I asked eagerly, with my heart ticking happily inside my chest.

The man frowned and rubbed his jaw. He had a pencil in the same hand he done it with. "Whitlaw?" he asked.

"Yes, sir. I come a long way to find that family. I even come across Riley's Ridge."

He sort of leaned over the little counter then and looked me up from my old brogans to the top of my head. "Riley's Ridge," he muttered. I reckon he knowed then that I'd been riding the rails and was a hobo boy.

"Hummm . . . I haven't been here too long myself. But I've heard there is an old ramshackle place out past town known as the Whitlaw place. Don't know if anyone but stray cats lives there anymore. Used to be an old lady out there."

"No, sir!" I said firmly, shaking my head. "They wouldn't be no old lady living there. Leastways not *too* old. She'd be about old enough to have a boy my age."

He studied me. "That right? Well, son, I guess you'll just have to go out there and find out for yourself."

"Could you tell me in what direction I should go?" I asked.

By the time he had finished telling me, they was a lady behind me, huffing and puffing as loud as them trains had, waiting to get up to the cage. Finally she exploded, "Will you hurry up? I want to buy a ticket!"

"Better step aside, son, so I can sell this lady a ticket," the agent told me. I thanked him and walked away with the woman giving me an impatient look.

Here I am, finally in Mill Springs, I thought as I walked along the street away from the depot. But in all that happiness, I still wished Abiah was with me, still wished old Mutt Dog was tramping along at my heels. Wherever Abiah was, I prayed for the thousandth time that she would be all right, safe and happy and warm.

I stuck my hand into my pocket and felt for my tooth. I wished I could glue it back in place so my ma wouldn't have to see me all snaggle-toothed and I wished I didn't have my nice knit cap and scarf stole from me and been beat up. It sure would be nice to have my ma see me looking sharp as a tack. But I hoped she would accept me in whatever condition I showed up in.

The ticket agent had told me the Whitlaw place he knowed of was about to fall apart. Well, I wouldn't believe it! The place my ma lived in would be all bright and cheerful, painted to a white gleam, just like the snow, I reckoned.

As I walked along, I gandered the street real good. It were clean and quiet with the smell of pastries floating out from somewhere. They was a huge fir tree right in the center of an intersection with a little picket fence running all around it. They wasn't no decorations on the tree, but it looked beautiful just the way it was. Looked like it might of growed up to be big right there in that spot and the town just growed around it. I stopped in front of the Five & Dime store and peered into the winder. They was some washboards standing up against a box that had soap cakes in it and they was big red ribbons tied onto the washboards. It looked so funny, I had to laugh. They was Christmas tree decorations and all kinds of stuff displayed. Even men's and women's hats. They was little pictures in gold frames that looked right pretty. I wished I had the money to buy my ma a present and take it to her.

Before I left the winder, I spit in my hands and tried to rub off all the dirt from my face. Then I flattened down my hair and tried to comb it as best I could with my fingers. I weren't much to look at in that condition, but I was the best I could do.

By the time I got outside town, in the direction the ticket agent give me, I was whistling a ditty. Every time I blowed out a whistle, my breath come rolling back to me in a cloudy puff. They was a sharp coldness that stung at the air and burned my cheeks, but I didn't care. Soon I'd be in my ma's house sitting in front of her warm fireplace with her and she'd have hot soup on the stove and muffins in the oven. A feller couldn't hardly be too cold thinking about all that.

I turned a little corner and there it was! The gleaming white house I'd thought about as Ma's. It had a wide porch that went all around it and they was some rocking chairs on it and a big wreath on the door. Oh, it was Ma's house all right!

Ma! I cried out inside me as I run toward it and raced up to the porch. Ma! My heart thundered like wild horses trailing across it! I raised my hand to knock on the door, but I stopped. The sound of piano music tinkled from the house and with it a female's voice singing.

"He saillllled oooover the ooooocean . . .
Taaaaking with him myyyy deeeevotion . . . "

Ma! It had to be Ma playing and singing! I sniffed so hard I drew back all the tears that was ready to fall, and raised my hand again. This time I knocked and the music stopped. I breathed deep, trying to keep calm, trying not to shake, trying to think of what I was going to say when she opened the door. Then I heard the click! I saw the doorknob turn. My mouth went dry. I felt like I'd turned to a stone.

"Hello," the pleasant voice of a girl about my age said and she smiled. She had long, blond-colored hair that lay across her shoulders and fell over the white lace dress she wore. They was a blue bow in her blond curls that matched the color of her eyes. She was some stranger that didn't belong there! Only Ma belonged there, opening the door for me, welcoming me into the house!

"Ah . . . " was the only noise that come out of my throat as I stared at the girl.

"Is there something you want?" the girl asked and I noticed she run her eyes over my dirty clothes and hair. But not in a cruel way. They seemed to be a kindness about her.

I cleared my throat. "The Whitlaws. I want the Whitlaws," I blurted out in a trembling voice.

"This isn't the Whitlaw place," she said.

"Well . . . well . . . I'm looking for . . . I'm looking for my ma . . . I mean, my mother." I struggled the words out, sounding like a croaking frog, not even listening to what she said.

A sadness fell over the girl's face. "I'm sorry. There isn't any mother in this house."

My mouth fell open and I stared at her. What do you *mean*, no mother in this house? This is the Whitlaw place! *Where is my ma?*

"My mother passed away two years ago," the girl went on. "Our last name is Frapart. I'm Tamara Lynn Frapart."

I shook my head and backed away from the door. "I . . . I . . ."

My heart was pounding so hard I felt like I would faint dead over. No! No! I wanted to shout. My ma ain't dead! And you ain't supposed to be living here and telling me these things! Finally I gained my courage and my voice back enough to tell her who I was and how far I'd come to be with my ma. She assured me that her ma couldn't be mine. Then she said, "There is a Whitlaw family living in Mill Springs. At least there used to be. I don't know if they still live here or not. Their place is about two miles more down the road."

My heart brightened then and broke into a joy of relief. I had to grin. Why, sure. I'd come to the wrong house, that was all. Ma's place would be just as nice, only a little further to walk. I thanked the girl as I ran down the steps and headed back onto the road. I commenced to whistle again and to feel the heaviness in me float away.

Chapter Eighteen

It didn't take long to walk two miles. But all along the way I noticed the houses got further and further apart and each one looked more tumbledown than the last one. They was names on the mailboxes and I read them off as I got close to them. Well, I told myself, it didn't mean nothing that all them houses was all wore out and junky looking. Ma's house would be just like the big gleaming house I first went to. It would even have a pretty wreath on the door . . .

After a while I come to the most tumbledown-looking shack on the road. It sat off behind a wobbly old fence that was half falling down and had a trellis over the gate. It looked like roses might of growed over the trellis in some long-ago time. I stood at the gate, staring downheartedly at the old weather-beaten clapboard house and the ugly weeds in the yard. They was a tilted post standing beside the gate that used to hold a mailbox. They couldn't be a soul living here, I thought.

Don't let this be the Whitlaw place, I prayed as I pushed the rotting gate open and walked to the house. I went to one of the dingy-looking winders and peered inside. The room looked deserted except for some old dusty-looking furniture and cobwebs everywhere. I moved my eyes around until they come to a fireplace made out of stones. They was a small fire in it, almost burning itself out. They *had* to be someone there!

I left the winder and hurried to the front door and knocked on it, but no one come to it. I rushed to another winder and then is when I seen an old woman sitting in a rocking chair. She had gray hair falling out of a bun all around her thin, wrinkled face and her lips was moving like she was mumbling things to herself. Her eyes was closed and her hands was resting in her lap with her long fingers trembling over each other. I studied her good. She *couldn't* be my ma. She was too old.

I went back to the door and knocked on it again. But the old lady didn't come. I turned the doorknob. It was loose and rattly and the door come creaking open. I stuck my head inside the room and looked around. The place smelled like it hadn't been cleaned up in a coon's age. The little bit of furniture in it was loaded with dust and powder from the fireplace. I pushed the door open a little more and called out, "Hello, ma'am!" The old lady didn't answer. I went inside and walked into the first open door I seen. The floor creaked under my feet as I walked. I stopped in the doorway and seen the old lady sitting there. Her eyes was still closed and her lips was still moving, mumbling something over and over. I listened a good while, trying to make it out, and finally it come to me that she was saying, "I am God's perfect child . . . I am God's perfect child." Just saying that, over and over.

I went up to her, but she didn't act like she even heard me. "Ma'am," I said, but she didn't open her eyes. Just kept up that mumbling and twiddling her fingers round and round. I reached out real cautious-like and touched her shoulder lightly and said, "Ma'am," again. She opened her eyes then and looked up at me. Her eyes was the lightest, lightest blue I ever seen.

"Ma'am, I was wondering. Could you be a Whitlaw?" I asked and it seemed like them blue eyes flashed with a little spark of life. "Are you a Whitlaw?" I repeated louder.

She sort of turned to stare up at me and her hands stopped moving. "Ain't no Whitlaws here. Used to be. Ain't been in a long time."

Used to be . . . ain't been in a long time! I felt my mouth go dry just like it done when I was on the porch of that pretty, shining house. I commenced to shake a little, too. "W–Where did they go?" I asked and my voice was shaking too.

"Went away. Went away somewhere. Don't recall where. Just left off from here."

"Could you maybe think of the place, if you was to try real hard? It's important to me and I come a long ways to see . . . " I had to stop and gulp. "To see my ma."

"Your ma?" she said like she didn't understand.

"I heard tell she was a Whitlaw."

Them old blue eyes studied me hard. "Miz Whitlaw, she had two boys and a girl. Took them with her. Weren't no other young'uns," she said and pressed her lips together like that was the end of it.

Yes, they was! I wanted to shout out. They was *me! I'm* her son! But instead I just sighed and looked down at the floor.

"Whitlaws is gone . . . " she mumbled and I looked up at her.

"Who are you, ma'am?" I asked her.

"Lisbeth Peterson. The Whitlaws let me stay with them. I helped with the young'uns. They was Brenda, Wyatt, and Robert."

Robert! For a minute I couldn't figure it out. Robert? But *I'm* Robert. Then Lisbeth said, "Robert, he was the oldest, the firstborn. Then they was Wyatt and Brenda. Took care of Robert from when he was a little tyke. Watched them all grow up."

The firstborn? No! I wanted to tell her. *I* was the firstborn! She give the second Robert *my* name! All at once it come to me—she give him my name because she never forgot me! She give me up, but she couldn't forget about me! I felt my throat squeeze up. I had to rub my hand across my eyes and hold it there so's the tears wouldn't spill out. My ma hadn't forgot me!

"What's wrong with you, boy?" Lisbeth asked and I moved my hand away from my eyes and sniffed.

"N–Nothing, ma'am. I was just wondering if . . . if I could maybe fix you a good fire before I go. And maybe I could get you something to eat. You look mighty alone here. Don't appear like you've had no help ner nothing around here."

"Ain't et in a while," she said like the thought of food made her come alive a little. "Had a boy to fix the fire for me, but he don't come much."

"You got any food around here?"

"Some in the pantry," she answered and I hurried away to find the pantry. As I crossed the room I heard her start mumbling, "I am God's perfect child," all over again.

Well, after I got the fire set good and give her something to eat, I'd be ready to head out again. They had to be someone in Mill Springs who knowed where the Whitlaws went. I'd just have to keep on moving until I found where it was. It sure was hard to let go of my dream of being with my ma on Christmas day. I'd thought about it and planned on it for so long, it all seemed like it was as much a part of me as my own arms was. I reckon no feller could give up his own arms without feeling the pain of it.

The pantry was a little off the kitchen. It looked pretty well stocked with canned vegetables and fruits in jars on the shelfs. Looked like Ma had left the old lady enough food. I took down a jar of peaches, carried it out to the kitchen, and opened it. Then I found a bowl in the cupboard and poured the peaches into it. They was a spoon on the counter so I poked that into the bowl. I et what was left of the peaches with my fingers and drunk all the juice that was in the jar. I looked at the peaches in the bowl, but decided it wouldn't be right to eat Lisbeth's part even if I could of. Before I took it in to Lisbeth, I stopped in the front room to stoke up the fire a little. When it was going good, I took the peaches in and handed the bowl to Lisbeth.

"How come you not to leave with the Whitlaws?" I asked her as she gobbled the peaches down.

"Wanted me to . . . but I had to stay. Mill Springs, it's my home. I used to live up the road till my house burned to the ground. I growed up here. Too old to move someplace else. Ain't got that much life left in me, no way."

"When did the Whitlaws leave?"

"Mr. Whitlaw, he got him a job somewhere and they left. But I don't recollect when it were," Lisbeth answered as she swallered the last peach and licked the spoon. Then she turned the bowl up and drunk the juice plumb out of it and handed it to me. "Much obliged," she said.

"Well, if you *could* remember, it sure would mean a lot to me,

Lisbeth," I told her, but she couldn't remember from one day to the next, seemed like. Fact of the matter was she didn't always make too much sense in what she said.

After I took the bowl to the kitchen and come back, I told her I was going to leave. She give me a frown and said, "You got to stay. See the fire don't go out. Gets cold. You got to stay till George comes home."

"Who is George?" I asked her.

"My husband. George Washington. He were our President, you know."

Alls I could say to that was, "Oh," and let it go.

She kept after me to stay until finally I told her I would stay the night and make sure the fire didn't go out. That seemed to please her. I reckoned I needed to be in a warm place to sleep for a change, anyway. Then it come to me that I ought to cut down a Christmas tree for Lisbeth, just like as if she was my ma. I remembered what the old clock man had said about taking kindness and passing it on. I reckoned Lisbeth could use some kindness just about as much as anyone could.

So that's what I done. I went out into the woods behind the house and found a fir tree that weren't exactly tall and weren't exactly short and weren't exactly just right, neither. It kind of tilted to the side and it didn't have a lot of branches. But it was the best I could find that weren't as tall as a house. I hacked it down with a rusty old ax I found in the yard and when I come dragging it through the front door of the house, Lisbeth was standing there in a baggy old dress and a baggy old sweater with her stockings rolled just above her ankles, watching me. Her face was all lit up with puzzled surprise.

"It's Christmas Eve, Lisbeth," I told her as I drug the tree near to the fireplace.

"Christmas Eve? Christmas Eve . . . ?" she repeated and I seen tears come into them old blue eyes.

"I'll get some wood and make a stand for it. You got any nails?" I asked as I laid the tree down.

"Ought to be some in the pantry," she answered and turned to stare down at the tree.

I went into the pantry and found the nails in an old rusty can on a shelf. Then I went outside and looked around for some small pieces of wood. I found a couple that had fell away from the house. They looked like they would do. I took them inside and while I hammered the wood into a cross with the ax handle, Lisbeth started talking a blue streak, just like she was coming out of a deep sleep and just realized what was going on.

"It smells good, that tree does. Smells like Christmas. Smells like a house ought to smell around here . . ."

"Christmas is tomorrow," I told her, hammering away on the cross.

"Used to have stockings hanging, always had them on the mantel . . . Christmas . . . time goes by too fast for me to keep up. Is it Christmas already?"

I glanced up at her. "Tomorrow," I said.

On and on she talked, and once, when I could get a word in, I asked, "Lisbeth, what is my . . . I mean, what is Miz Whitlaw's name?" I kept right on hammering.

"Her name? June. It be June Rose Whitlaw," she said and she went right back to talking about whatever jumped into her head.

June Rose Whitlaw . . . June Rose . . . it sounded like a summer name, a sunshine name . . . a bright, cheerful name. For some reason I wanted to lay down and cry just to think about that name. But I kept on hammering on the cross until I had it fixed and all set for the tree. When I was ready, Lisbeth helped me hold it steady while I nailed the cross to the bottom of it. When I stood it up, it looked about as bedraggled as any Christmas tree ever could, even worse than when I drug it in. Seemed like the spindly branches sagged more and the tiny needles was already dropping off of it. I moved back and studied it. Then I snuck a guilty look at Lisbeth, thinking how disappointed she had to be over it. Her hands was covering her mouth and her eyes was as big as saucers. I gulped and started to say how sorry I was. Then she moved her hands away from her mouth and said, "Lord . . . Lord, ain't it beautiful!"

I looked back at the tree. Then back at Lisbeth. Her eyes was shining like stars and there was a big smile on her face then. It sure didn't take much to make the old lady happy.

"You got any decorations for the tree, Lisbeth?" I asked her.

"No . . . no decorations. None a'tall," she answered, still staring at the tree.

I thought for a minute. "Well, you got any newspapers?"

She turned and looked at me. "Got some magazines."

She told me where the magazines was and I found them, a good stack of them, in a corner of a dusty, spidery room that looked like it might of been a bedroom at one time. I picked up a handful and some granddaddy spiders run out from between the pages and hurried off across the floor. I looked around the room, thinking maybe my ma had slept there. Maybe she woke in the mornings and looked out the winder and watched the sun come up. I went to the winder and looked out. It faced the woods and I could imagine the sun shining down through the tops of the trees in the early mornings, casting shadders across the yard and house.

Or maybe, I thought, it was the "other" Robert's bedroom. Maybe he woke there with his brother and they had piller fights and jumped out the winder sometimes and run down into the woods playing hide-and-seek. Maybe they . . .

Well, wasn't no use in thinking about all that, I decided as I left the room. They was gone. Looked like I weren't meant to be with my ma. Leastways not for now. I reckoned I had me a gran'ma instead.

Me and Lisbeth sat down at the kitchen table and tore pictures out of the magazines, cars and flowers and houses and cats and anything we could find that was colorful.

"Here's a dog's face . . . always liked pets . . . most especially dogs," Lisbeth said as she ripped out a picture of a bulldog's mean-looking face.

"I had me a dog once. I called him Mutt Dog. I dearly loved him," I told her as I bent over a magazine. Thinking about Mutt Dog made me get a lump in my throat and I had to clear it.

Lisbeth looked up at me. "What breed were he?"

"I reckon he were a mix between a mutt and a mutt," I said and we had a little chuckle.

"Where is he? Is he out in the yard?"

"No, ma'am. He's dead," I said. And I wanted to die myself just having to say the word.

I went back to ripping pictures out of the magazines, finding all I could that looked cheery. After a little I realized Lisbeth was staring at me and I looked up. They was a puzzled frown on her face.

"Who are you, son? You from around here? You live up the road? Was you here last week?"

That's when I told her where I'd come from and a little about the Hicksons and how I'd traveled to get to Mill Springs. Seemed like I ought to tell her, seeing as how we was working together, and with the Christmas tree waiting to be decorated and the fire going good in the fireplace, it was the friendly thing to do.

"Thought you was from up the road aways. Well . . . how come you to want to come here so bad?"

I had to think on that a minute. Finally I said, "I reckon you could say I'm a distant relative of the Whitlaws. I was hoping to see them."

She sat back in her chair and stared at me a little then said, "I declare, you do hold a look on your face like the oldest boy, Robert. Yes, I can see it." She went back to scanning the pages of the magazines and we didn't say no more.

When we had enough bright, pretty pictures tore out of the magazines we took them into the front room and commenced to punch holes in them and stick them on the Christmas tree branches. As we did it I said, "I got a friend I been looking for."

"Good . . . good to have a friend . . . you're my friend," she said and she looked over at me and smiled. She seemed more like a little kid right then than she did an old lady.

"Well," I said and took a deep breath, "I reckon it's time you knowed your friend's name. I'm Robert."

Lisbeth turned and squinted her eyes at me. "Now you ain't the

Whitlaw Robert, are you?" she asked and pursed her lips and continued to stare at me like maybe I was him and was playing a joke on her.

"No, ma'am, I'm . . . well, I'm just Robert."

"It's a good name, Robert is. Common, but good."

"It ain't fancy like my friend's name is, that's for sure. Her name is Abiah."

"Abiah . . . Abiah . . ." she repeated and turned back to the tree and shoved a picture of a bright blue roadster onto a branch.

"I miss Abiah," I said after a while and Lisbeth didn't say anything. She was too busy shoving pictures onto the tree branches.

When we was all finished, we stood back and stared at the tree. It looked even more bedraggled and strange with all them pictures out of magazines twisted and turned and drooping on them already drooping branches. But Lisbeth clapped her hands together and cried out how beautiful it was, so I tried to see it the way she did. Only I couldn't. Reckon I was comparing it to the Hicksons' Christmas tree. The Hicksons had a bright star at the top of their tree. That old ugly bulldog face from out of the magazine sat at the top of *this* tree!

"I got to go now, Lisbeth," I told her after she had made some tea and sandwiches and we sat in the kitchen eating and drinking.

"No . . . no, you stay here," she said. "Keep the fire going. You stay," she insisted.

Well, it was getting dark and that meant it was getting colder outside. I told her I'd stay and leave in the morning.

I slept on the floor close to the fireplace with an old scratchy army blanket Lisbeth give me to cover me up. Before she went to her bedroom she said, "I got some money, Robert. Tomorrow you go to town and buy us a Christmas cake. Bakery'll be open till noon. You buy us a nice walnut cake for Christmas day."

I was too worn out to argue with her, to tell her I wouldn't be there, so I just said, "Yes, ma'am," and snuggled down into that old scratchy blanket and looked at the fire.

Chapter Nineteen

Robert, you got to get up now! Robert! Cake! Christmas cake at the bakery!" I heard Lisbeth's voice coming briskly into my ears and I opened my eyes. "It's near to ten o'clock, Robert. We have to have our Christmas cake!" There was something different in the way she sounded. It was like she come out of a long, dead sleep and woke up crackling with energy.

I sat up. I hadn't slept to ten o'clock in my whole life! Lisbeth had gone on out to the kitchen. I smelled strong coffee and got up, shoving my hair back out of my face, and follered her. When I got to the kitchen I seen she had a cup of coffee and a biscuit setting at the table for me. I washed up real fast at the sink and hurried to the table.

"Eat quick and drink your coffee. It's cold today. Colder than yesterday. Johnny Cook won't unlock the door for no one after he closes at noon. Never would. Closes the bakery door and locks it at twelve noon of Christmas Day. Goes home to his family. Hurry now, Robert."

I started to say something about me leaving, but she seemed so excited about that Christmas cake, I thought I might as well go and get it for her. "Yes, ma'am, Lisbeth," I said and I whipped into that biscuit and washed it down with the hot coffee. Before I was finished swallering, she was counting change out on the table to pay for the cake. I wiped my mouth on my sleeve and got up, scooped the change off the table into my pocket, and started buttoning my coat.

"You'll not be able to miss Johnny Cook's Bakery, Robert. The sign in front is red and yeller and proclaims the name to the whole street."

"Yes, ma'am," I said and started for the door.

"Robert . . . Merry Christmas," Lisbeth said.

I turned around and she was smiling real big at me. I smiled back and said, "Merry Christmas, Lisbeth."

Well, I thought as I bounded down the road with my breath shooting out like a fog in front of me and scrunching my neck down into the collar of my coat, trying to keep warm, here I am in Mill Springs and it's Christmas day. Only it ain't nothing like I expected it to be. I ain't with my ma. I'm with an old lady that sometimes don't seem right in her head and other times she seems real right in her head. I'd come all this way for a big letdown. I sniffed, trying to keep from bawling. Then, real fast, I slung my shoulders back, raised my neck out of my coat collar, lifted my head, and looked straight ahead. I was thirteen years old. I had to act it.

When I come to the big gleaming white house where I'd first stopped to see if my ma lived there, I looked at it with a longing in my heart. Not for me. For my ma. Wherever she was, I wished she was living in such a house. And wherever Abiah was, I wished she was in a warm, clean, good place like that house looked to be. While I was staring at it, the front door opened and that girl that give me the name of Tamara

Lynn come out and give me a wave of her hand. "Merry Christmas!" she called to me. And before I could say it back to her, she said, "Did you find your mother?"

I started to call back that I hadn't. Then for some reason I said, "No. I found my gran'ma, though!"

"That's wonderful!" Tamara Lynn said with a smile.

Well, to be truthful, I reckon it was pretty wonderful. If a feller can't find his ma, the next-best thing to that would be to find his gran'ma. Of course Lisbeth weren't my *true* gran'ma. But she was the next-best to it. I felt a quick flood of happiness as I went on down the road and turned toward town.

Lisbeth was right. Johnny Cook's Bakery sign was so big it couldn't be missed. And the aroma coming from it was something no one could miss. It set between other shops that was closed and had MERRY CHRISTMAS and HAPPY YULETIDE signs in the winders. The street was near about deserted except for a truck or two going by with big green Christmas trees in the back.

I opened the bakery door and walked inside. The sweet, doughy smells that hit me in the face was so good they could of knocked me plumb out. I looked around. They was a small Christmas tree setting on one end of the glass counter case with an angel on the top. She had long white hair that flowed all the way down into the branches and colored balls and tiny figures made out of wood hanging all over. They was even some little red bows tied here and there in the branches. It sure put the tree me and Lisbeth decorated to shame.

My eyes left the tree and swung down to the pastries that was inside the glass case. Soon as I seen them my mouth commenced to water.

They was cupcakes and muffins with globs of frosting on them and cookies cut out in the shapes of stars and Christmas trees and angels with bright sprinkles of red and green sugar on them and cakes with coconut toppings nested in mounds of snow-white frosting and plumpy doughnuts with a thick glaze on them. I reckoned if them things didn't all sell out before noon, something had to be wrong with the townfolks!

While I stood there eyeing everything, a man come out from a doorway behind the counter and said with a pleasant smile, "What can I do for you, young feller?"

I reckoned him to be Johnny Cook. He wore a white apron over his big belly and had on a white shirt with a blue patterned necktie. The top of his head was all shiny bald. But he had hair around the sides that fluffed out over his ears. He didn't look too old so I reckoned he got bald early.

"I come to buy a cake for Miz Lisbeth Peterson," I answered him.

"That'll be a walnut cake with chocolate icing. Lisbeth won't have no other kind on Christmas day. I thought she might of forgot this year, though, her being not always too clear in her mind," he said as he bent down to pull a beautiful cake with a dark icing and sprinkles of walnuts on top out from the glass case. "Made special this morning as a matter of fact," he added as he set the cake on the counter and beamed proudly over it.

I pulled the change Lisbeth give me out of my pocket. "It sure does look good," I told Johnny Cook.

"How is Lisbeth? She hadn't gone and lost her mind all the way yet, has she?" he asked.

"A little. Seems like a little," I answered as I laid the money on the counter.

Johnny Cook smiled and picked up the change. "I reckon she hadn't. Still able to count out the correct change for the cake." He dropped the money into the cash register then leaned over the counter. "How'd you come to be picking up this cake for her? I ain't seen you before."

I told him, but not about me being the Whitlaw woman's firstborn son. I reckoned they weren't no point in doing that. But they was some questions I had to ask. "Sir, did you know the Whitlaw family that Lisbeth lived with?" I asked and waited hard for his answer.

"Sure. Knowed them well. Kids usta come in here," he answered and I cut right into the next question.

"What was Miz Whitlaw like?"

"June Rose? Fine good woman. Took good care of her young'uns. Good wife, too. The Whitlaws always paid their bills even when this depression struck the country, they did. After a while they just plain couldn't do it. No work around here. Nelson, he was a first-rate carpenter. Too bad they had to move on. Don't know where they went to. Seems like, from what I heard, they started moving around a lot. Just sort of got lost in the country somehere, you might say."

"W–what did Miz June Rose Whitlaw look like?" I shouldn't of asked it, but I couldn't keep from it. He looked at me and frowned, like it were peculiar for me to ask.

"Matter of fact she had just about the same coloring you have and even the same colored hair. The boys, they had it too. But the little girl, she was blond like her daddy."

Same coloring and same color of hair. June Rose and me . . . my ma and me . . . same coloring, same hair. . . . It come like a Christmas blessing for me to know that.

I didn't have a chance to ask nothing else because Johnny Cook changed the subject. "You been helping Lisbeth out, have you?"

"Yes, sir. A little."

"Well, the poor old woman needs someone out there with her. She should of gone with the Whitlaws when they left, and they sure wanted her to, but she was too stubborn. She claimed to have been born in this town and she would die here too. Wouldn't budge an inch. How long you going to stay out there with her?"

"Well, I ain't aiming to stay. I'm planning on leaving today. Right after I take this cake to Lisbeth," I answered.

Johnny Cook moved hisself back from leaning on the counter and frowned deeply at me. "Why, son, you can't leave on Christmas day! Wouldn't it near about do that poor old woman in to have you do that! You ought to stay the week at least."

Then I frowned. "Well . . . I dunno . . ."

"You got somewhere else to go?"

"Well, not right away . . ."

"To tell you the truth, folks in town here would be willing to pitch in and pay someone to stay out there and do for Lisbeth. We been talking on it for sometime now. Will you think on it?"

I took in a deep breath. "Yes, sir," I answered. Well, it sure is a temptation, I thought. With a little bit of money I could get around a lot easier. I wouldn't have to go hungry and I could go on looking for my ma and Abiah, too.

"You'll be needing a box for that cake," Johnny Cook said and he turned his head toward the door behind the counter and shouted, "*You, girl! Abby!* Bring me one of them small cake boxes out here!"

Abby . . . Abby . . . I won't never hear that name and not think of Abiah, I thought wistfully. While Johnny Cook's head was turned, I snuck my finger along the edge of that fine chocolate walnut cake and scooped off a little of the frosting to poke into my mouth. I'd just got the sweet taste of it on my tongue when someone come stomping out of the back room, making all kinds of racket, and tossed a box on the counter.

"I *done told* you, mister! My name *ain't Abby!* It's *Abiah!* It's all I got to call my own and I *ain't* going to let no one take it away from me!"

I swallered that frosting so fast I near about choked on it! Was I hearing my ears right? That name, the voice, the very words I'd heard before! *It had to be Abiah Ringer!* I moved my head a little and craned my neck so's I could see around Johnny Cook.

"Watch your temper, girl! No need to get riled up on Christmas day," Johnny Cook said and it didn't sound like he was angry at all.

He moved a little to the left and I moved my head some more. Then I seen her. She was wearing a dirty apron and her short, stringy hair was flopped down into her eyes and her face was all pinched up, mad as a hornet, looking right into Johnny Cook's eyes just like he'd already gone and stole the only thing she owned in the world.

"*Abiah! Abiah! It's you!*" I cried.

A stunned look come over her face and she looked around slowly to gander across the counter. When she seen me standing there staring at her, her mouth fell wide open. "Abiah!" I cried again. "It's *me!* Robert!"

"Robert!" she said real low. Then it just exploded right out of her in a loud whoop. "ROBERT!" She rushed around the counter as I moved toward the end of it. Then we stopped and stared at each other. Is it *really* you, Abiah? I wondered way down deep in my heart. Is it really you, after all this time? From the look on her face, it seemed like she was thinking the same thing about me.

"Are you all right, Abiah?" I asked her and my heart commenced to thunder for fear she weren't all right, that some great harm had come to her, so terrible that she would never forget it.

"I'm all right," she answered. "I'm fine as could be, Robert."

"Are you *sure*, Abiah? Tell me the truth!" But even as I asked her to tell me the truth, I feared what she would tell me.

She commenced to laugh. "I done said I was, didn't I?"

"Abiah . . . Abiah . . . " It were all I could say then and I opened my arms to her and she walked into them and we pressed close and I wanted to cry into her old, messy, stringy hair. I heard her sniff next to my ear and I knowed she might be crying or ready to. I didn't want to let go of her but I heard Johnny Cook clear his throat and I let her go.

"How did you get here, Abiah?" I asked her as we stood there looking at each other.

"I just kept on coming north, like we was going to together. I knowed you'd keep on coming. I got here and watched all the trains that come in, but I never did see you. I knowed you'd come, though. I knowed we'd see each other again. Are you mad at me because I couldn't jump off the train, Robert?" she asked with her face suddenly all dark.

"No, Abiah, I ain't mad. I knowed you couldn't jump. I never held nothing against you for that," I told her.

Suddenly Abiah frowned and looked around the floor. "Where is Mutt Dog?" she asked and she went to the front winder and looked out. When she turned around she had a question on her face.

"He drownded, Abiah. Mutt Dog drownded," I answered softly and the memory of it made me live it all over again.

Abiah's face crumpled up for a second like she was going to cry, but she didn't. "Poor old Mutt Dog. He were a good friend," she said and come back to where I was standing.

I felt so bad seeing the look of pain on her face, that I spoke right up. "But maybe he ain't really dead, Abiah. I mean, I ain't for certain that he died. Who knows, he might show up someday. I heard tell of dogs doing that, of running all across the country and just showing up one day right out of the blue."

"You reckon Mutt Dog could do that?" Abiah asked hopefully, and her face brightened.

"I found you, didn't I?" I said, and she smiled.

"When did you get here, Robert?" she asked then.

I told her as quick as I could with Johnny Cook standing there listening to us. Reckoned he took in my whole life story in two minutes just about! But he was fixing the cake in the box and didn't act like he was paying no mind.

"Come out to Lisbeth's with me, Abiah," I said finally.

"I can't, Robert. Not now. I got to clean up the kitchen and wash up all the cake and pie pans and . . ."

"It's Christmas," Johnny Cook spoke up. "Reckon them pans can wait till tomorrow."

Abiah's face brightened as we both looked at Johnny Cook's big smile. "You will be back tomorrow, won't you, *Abiah?*" He put a little emphasis on her name and I could tell Abiah was right pleased about that.

"Oh, yes, sir. And thank you, sir," Abiah said as she whipped off her apron and run to the back room. When she come back, she was wearing the red coat and pushing her hair out of her face.

Johnny Cook handed the box with the cake in it across the counter to me. "Might be," he said, "that Lisbeth could use a girl's help out at her place just about as much as she needs your help, son. You might mention it to her. Tell her Johnny Cook said Abiah is a good little dishwasher and floor sweeper. Oh, and tell her Merry Christmas for me, too. And you kids, have a good Christmas." They was a good wide, friendly smile on his face when he said all that. It sure did make my heart warm up to him.

Abiah and me thanked him and wished him a Merry Christmas. After we got outside the door Abiah stared at my mouth and said, "You lost a tooth, Robert."

I told her how it happened and a few other things, saving the most for later. But I didn't mention about my ma. Not yet. She told me how one old hobo took to her like she was his own blood child, protected her and got her food and wouldn't let no one cuss around her ner nothing. It sure give me relief to know that. As we walked along the road to Lisbeth's place she said, "I thought about you every day, Robert. And I never give up hope of seeing you again. I thought about you real hard yesterday."

"How come?" I asked.

"Because it was your birthday, silly. Didn't you remember?"

Then she started in to asking me a hundred questions about my ma and "what's she like?" and "do you like her a lot?" and such. When I told her I didn't get to see my ma she looked disappointed and said, "Oh, Robert, you come all this way."

"I ain't give up," I said firmly. "I won't ever give up on looking for her. Same as I looked for you. And the same as you looked for me. I'll find her, too. I know I will. But listen, Abiah. I found me a gran'ma that knowed her, even took care of her young'uns."

"Is she the Lisbeth you and Johnny Cook mentioned?"

"Yes. And she's a sweet old thing. You'll like her. She don't always make a lot of common sense, but her good heart makes up for it."

Abiah still looked disappointed. "Don't be sad," I told her. "Be glad that I found me a gran'ma. I ain't never had one before."

She smiled then and we stopped on the road with the mist beginning to fall and looked into each other's eyes. "You was my Christmas present all along, Abiah," I told her as I watched the mist sprinkle into her hair. "It weren't my ma I was meant to have for my gift. It were you." Then I raised her damp hair off her cheek and kissed her softly there.

"And you are my gift, Robert. The best Christmas gift I could ever wish for in a thousand years."

"Merry Christmas, Abiah," I told her.

"Merry Christmas, Robert," she said and I took her hand and held it as we started walking again.

A Note About the Author

"The sounds of trains, fast ones, slow ones, chugging-loud ones with blowing whistles and blasting steam. It all comes back to me when I hear the clatter of a train in the distance.

"I close my eyes and see things as they were: the house I lived in when I was a child, the fruit-packing shed and the railroad tracks across the road. . . . Everything I write comes from my childhood. And all the characters, no matter who they are, hold a little part of me inside them."

Patricia Pendergraft was born and raised in the San Joaquin Valley of California. The people in her world have inspired the memorable characters in her stories; those in *As Far As Mill Springs* have been inspired by the homeless people she watched as a child, hopping the trains as they moved back and forth over the tracks so close to her home.

"Someone said that we are a part of all that has gone before us, all that we have experienced throughout our lives. I believe this to be true for me as a writer."

Patricia Pendergraft, author of *Miracle at Clements Pond* and other novels for young people, now lives in Livermore, California. She has four children, Tammy, Theresa, Richard, and Heidi; and three grandchildren.